D1325169

You're the Best!

Stories about friendship

Selected by
Belinda Hollyer

KINGFISHER

KINGFISHER
An imprint of Kingfisher Publications Plc
New Penderel House, 283-288 High Holborn, London WC1V 7HZ
www.kingfisherpub.com

First published by Kingfisher 2006
1 3 5 7 9 10 8 6 4 2

This selection and introduction copyright © Belinda Hollyer 2006
The acknowledgements on page 224 constitute
an extension of this copyright page.

The moral right of the compiler, authors and illustrator has been asserted.

All rights reserved. No part of this publication may be
reproduced, stored in a retrieval system or transmitted
by any means electronic, mechanical, photocopying or
otherwise, without the prior permission of the publisher.

A CIP catalogue record for this
book is available from the British Library.

ISBN-13: 978 0 7534 1332 6
ISBN-10: 0 7534 1332 9

Printed in India
1TR/0406/THOM/SCHOY/80STORA/C

Contents

Introduction   5

Annie and Me   9
Libby Gleeson

Make Friends, Make Friends,   23
Never Never Break Friends
Julia Green

Toad Crossing   39
Frances Thomas

Under the Influence   55
Marcia Byalick

T4J   73
Sophie McKenzie

The Gardener's Daughter   92
Jamila Gavin

Speaking Esperanto   108
Shirley Klock

Dear Meena   122
Angela Kanter

The Middle Ground   136
Belinda Hollyer

The Swing Chair   150
Norman Silver

Silence   166
Lois Metzger

Taking Flight   179
Tessa Duder

The Alien   194
Sue Anderson

Eve Goes First   208
Sarah D. Bunting

Author Biographies   221

Acknowledgements   224

Introduction

Friendships matter a great deal to all the women I know: young girls, mature women, and at every point in between. Friends not only help to shape who we are, but they also play a large part in who we become. So they are equally important to young girls and to the women those girls will grow into. Families may torment you, boyfriends come and go, jobs can turn sour – but as some wise person said, true friends are the threads on which we string the beads of our lives.

Many boys and men also have close friendships, of course, but female friendships are distinctive because they are usually based on particular qualities, with emotional support and conversation at the top of the list! Such friendships are fed by laughter and confidences, and many of the highs (and the lows) of everyday life are enhanced (or soothed) simply by sharing them with a close friend. The worst of our problems are endured together with sympathy or floods of tears, while the best moments are marked by mutual delight and celebration.

Some people keep their friends apart and enjoy separate lives with each one, while others expect their close friends to get along with each other, no matter what. Like most things in life, friendships are a work in progress. They change in unforeseen ways, even if you don't want them to. A troubled or doomed friendship may sit like an elephant in a corner of the room, which no one mentions for fear of upsetting you. ("*Why* don't you ever have a friend over?" or, "Whatever happened to that *nice* friend of yours?") By contrast, however, you may be one of those people with a hundred very close friends constantly available. Either way, the chances are that you – the reader of this collection of stories – care a lot about your friends.

The writers of these stories celebrate friendship across five continents and in fourteen different ways, but all of them explore some of the circumstances that help such relationships tick or slow them down a bit. Here are friendships thriving in the best and the worst of times and those observed from a distance or felt firsthand. Here are stories about finding and losing best friends or about friends who betray you or let you down. Here are stories about making unexpected friends and about having no friends at all. There's even one about waiting patiently for an old friend to come to her senses and be a best friend again!

A real friendship can't be taken for granted. It needs care and attention from both sides, but with luck, it may last and grow. Is there anything good to be said for the passage of time? Here's one thing: it's the way your old friends get to experience the unfolding of the years along with you.

Belinda Hollyer

Belinda Hollyer has been a teacher, a school librarian and a children's book publisher, and is now a full-time writer and anthologist. This is her third anthology for Kingfisher; the others are poetry collections: **Haven't You Grown!** *and* **She's All That!** *Her first novel,* **The Truth about Josie Green**, *was published earlier this year.*

Annie and Me

LIBBY GLEESON

I met Annie on the first day of kindergarten. I was hanging on tightly to my sister's hand. Annie was on her own, standing in the area outside our classroom. I couldn't help thinking how brave she was to be there with no one else. No mum or dad. No big brother or sister. Not even a cousin or a neighbour. And she was shorter than me.

Inside, we had name tags. We were *Jenny Traill* and *Annie Tran* so we sat together. We stared at the charts with numbers, letters and bright colours and the poster of a rock pool with anemones and lots of shells. And then Mrs Donaldson asked us to put our hands up if we'd ever been outside Sydney. Lots of hands went up. I've been to Albury because Mum's sister lives there.

She said to keep our hands up if we'd ever been outside New South Wales. Some kids didn't understand what she meant. I did. I've been to Melbourne in Victoria because Mum's other sister lives there.

Then she said to keep our hands up if we'd

ever been outside Australia. Only mine and Annie's stayed up.

"Where have you been?" she hissed.

"New Zealand." My dad is from there and we go to stay with my grandparents for holidays.

"I win," she grinned. "I've been to Vietnam and Thailand and Hong Kong and America."

"Did you go to Disneyland?"

"Of course."

Everyone wanted to play with her at breaktime but she chose me. We ate together at lunchtime and she let me have a hold of her favourite shell, a black-and-white one that she had wrapped up in a tissue in her lunchbox. It was like a shiny, round ball that had been pushed out of shape and there was an opening, a slit, in one part of it. I couldn't see inside because the edges all folded in on themselves.

When the bell went at the end of the day, we stood holding hands until my sister came to pick me up.

"Who are you going home with?" she said to Annie.

"I'll be right." And Annie ran off through the gate at the other end of the playground.

That set the pattern for the year. Annie and Jenny became AnnieandJenny: one word, two bodies joined at the shoulder and hip. Arms entwined, we giggled our way through life as a three-legged adventure. We shared and swapped our pencils and crayons, our worksheets and our library books, our breaktime drinks of guava and orange and our lunches of spring rolls and salad sandwiches.

Annie came to play one Saturday afternoon. Under Mum and Dad's bed, we found the box that had all the Christmas decorations in it. We spent the afternoon decorating the chilli bush that stood a little bit higher than we did. We wove the tinsel and the paper chains through the branches and hung gold and silver baubles next to the blood-red fruit. We had to stand on the garden wall that Dad had built to reach the top. We wrapped up stones in coloured cellophane and piled these high around the trunk, like presents. Mum took a photo of us, sitting on the sandstone wall, one either side of our creation: the most beautiful thing we'd ever made.

That wall is in the middle of the backyard. Twenty-four heavy sandstone blocks. We lay on it, lizards, sunning ourselves in our swimming costumes after running under the hose. We performed on it, singing our hearts out to our adoring fans of dolls and teddies and my cat, Munchkin. We squatted behind it to put on puppet shows for Mum and Dad and it was our display wall where anything, stones or seeds, broken china, anything we found, could be lined up to show off to any audience.

On my tenth birthday we had a picnic at the beach park at Bronte. Mum and Dad went to do the cliff walk to Bondi but Annie and I stayed to swim and then to play around the rocks. We found lots of shells and we filled a plastic bag with seawater, so the tiny creatures wouldn't die, and took them home. Mine did die and ended up in a coffee jar in the toy box. When Annie's died, she cleaned them out and brought them round to make a display on the wall. She put those shells in a line, almost touching, coloured ones together, conical ones together and the flat, round, ridged ones side by side. In the centre she placed her zebra shell, black-and-white striped, shiny. They covered two of the sandstone blocks. She left them all there, except for that special one.

Her mum ran the corner shop in Addison Road and they lived in a flat above it. When Annie came to my place, we played in my room or on the wall, but when I went to her place, it was different. "Let's go up to Marrickville Road," she'd say and so we'd head for the Vietnamese shops and go through their plastic specials in the drums on the footpath. All the restaurant owners knew her and we could wander in and get a cool drink and she'd have a joke with them in her language, which I couldn't understand.

Annie's room was tiny and so we shared her bed, lying there listening to the aeroplanes taking off, telling each other the life stories of the passengers.

"There's a woman in the first class who's off to California to become a movie star and she's already got a part in five films and she's never coming back again. Her parents are really sad but she doesn't care."

"And there's a family who haven't seen their father for ten years since he went away, only now he's died and left them a million dollars in a bank in Hong Kong and they're going to get it."

"And there's this kid and she thought she was an orphan but now she's found out her mother is a princess in Paris and she's going to join her."

"But she can't speak French."

"She's having lessons on the way."

And then in Year Five, for the first time, Annie missed a day of school. She hadn't come over at the weekend because she said she had a headache. I sat by myself. At breaktime everyone asked where she was and I said she was just a bit off colour and she'd be back the next day. She wasn't. I had rung her on the first night but there was no answer. That was weird because her mother never closed the shop until really late. I wanted Mum or Dad to drive me over there, but they wouldn't, and they said I couldn't walk over by myself.

Annie came back on the third day. She had Band-Aids on the inside of both elbows and she boasted about how much blood was taken from there. "You can see it come out," she said, "filling up this syringe. It doesn't hurt." She shrugged then, and when we all asked her why, she said the doctor just wanted to check her blood. At lunchtime she said she was tired so we went to the library and climbed down into the reading pit.

By Friday, Annie was in hospital. Mum came and got me from school at lunchtime and said Annie's mum had just called her. Leukaemia.

"There'll be months and months of treatment," Mum said.

"But I can visit her."

"Not always. There'll be times when she's too sick and when no one can visit except her mum. She's a very sick little girl."

"Will I catch it?"

Mum shook her head.

"She will get better, won't she?"

Mum didn't answer me straight away. She started to say something about how things are better now than when she was a little girl. Words like *chemo-something,* and *survival,* but I was only half listening.

I wandered up the backyard and I lay on the wall, our wall, Annie's and mine, my cheek pressing against the grainy golden edge of the warm stone.

I had never been in a hospital before. No one in my family is ever sick. My shoes squeaked on the shiny vinyl floor as we walked down corridor after corridor. There were strange smells, too, that made me think of when it's my turn to clean the bath. Through half-open doors, I saw people gathered around beds, and sometimes people alone, their faces peering out towards the door, the sheets pulled up to their chins. Then we were in the children's section and a ward with a name I couldn't read. I wanted to turn and run away, but Mum put her hand on my shoulder and I had the feeling that, deep down, she wanted to run away too.

Annie was sitting up in bed, looking just like she always did. She grinned and waved as if she was really pleased to see us. There was a plastic tube coming off a tall stand beside the bed. Drops of something ran down that tube from a little plastic bag at the top. Then the tube ran up inside the sleeve of her pyjamas. I wanted to ask her where it went, but Mum was fussing around and asking Annie how her mum was and about how she was feeling and if the food was any good. I wanted to tell Mum to go away for a while and leave us and then I could ask about the tube, but the moment never came.

Annie wanted to know everything about school and so I told her how someone had nicked some money from the Year Six teacher's desk and the police had come and given the whole school a big lecture but no one had owned up. Everyone reckoned they knew who it was, but no one could prove it.

On the way home, Mum told me about the tube. She said there were drugs going into Annie's chest. Annie would have to be in hospital, off and on, for another few weeks, and she would get a lot sicker from all the drugs before she got better.

At the end of that week, Annie came home for three days. I went round to her place but I couldn't stay the night, because her mum wanted her to get a good night's sleep, and I suppose she thought that we'd talk all night, as usual. I was strangely glad not to stay and I didn't once ask her about the tubes.

When I got home I took a needle from Mum's sewing basket. I lay under the sheet and I pricked myself in the centre of my chest. Even when I shut my eyes as tight as tight, I couldn't make the needle go right in.

By Tuesday, Annie was back in hospital. Mum said the first lot of treatment hadn't worked as well as people had hoped and now it had to happen all over again. I wasn't allowed to visit this time. "You could take in an infection," Mum said.

I sat by myself all week. When people came near me, I pretended my book was really good and I didn't look up. If anyone wanted to know about Annie, I snapped back that I didn't know, and when Sonia Masters asked if she was going to die, I ran out of the playground and down Marrickville Road. Then I took the bus to the hospital.

The nurse on the desk told me that Annie was now in a different room and that I couldn't see her. She said no one was allowed in except her mother, but I could peep through a window if I wanted.

I stood on tiptoe and peered through the glass. Annie was asleep. Strands of her hair were on the pillow as if she had lain there and then turned away, leaving behind some memory of herself. There were dark purple patches under her eyes and pinkish blotches on her cheeks.

She was drowning in the sea of white starched sheets and hospital covers.

On the little cupboard next to the bed, beside a glass of water, was the zebra shell.

On the way home I thought of Sadako. *Sadako and the Thousand Paper Cranes.* We read it in Year Three and Annie's mum showed us how to make the cranes but neither of us was very good. I couldn't make cranes, and maybe they only worked in Japan and in Vietnam. Could I do something else? I pressed my nose against the glass, looking out at all the cars filled with healthy people heading off home from work.

I lay on the wall while the sun went down and shadows from the jacaranda tree stretched over me. I picked up one of the shells that Annie had placed there and it lay in the palm of my hand. I ran my thumb over the ridges that fanned out from the white base. They became darker and darker till, at the edges, they were almost black.

The next morning, after breakfast, I sat in my room with my photo album and searched for Annie. There we were, together at the beach, the park, in the garden, at the table for birthday parties, lined up in class, serious-faced or laughing and clowning around.

Dad came into the room. "I want you to come to the beach with me."

I shook my head. "I don't feel like it."

"A swim will do you good."

"I don't want to be 'done good'."

"C'mon." He dragged me to my feet.

We stood on the sand at Coogee. Dad, as usual, looked out at the island. "I reckon it moves," he said. "You coming in?"

I was staring at my feet. There was a double pipi there, washed clean, shiny in the sun.

"No. There's something I want to do here." I spread my towel and emptied the bag that held the sunscreen and water. He headed for the surf. I trawled the high-water line, kicking over the heavy black seaweed. I found small grey shells shaped like cones, turban-shaped shells with light blue whorls and more open pipis, the creatures in them long gone. I couldn't bring myself to prise free those shells that clung to the edges of the rock pool but I found empty oyster shells, and others that I didn't recognise, discarded on the sand.

As he towelled himself, Dad looked at my collection but didn't say anything. That night I rinsed the sand from each shell and placed them all along the wall. They covered another of the sandstone blocks.

Annie grew sicker and sicker. Mum and Dad watched in silence as my line of shells grew longer and longer. Her hair fell out in great clumps, and every Saturday I returned to Coogee. Her mouth filled with ulcers, and I walked the length of the beach, gathering. Her skin grew red and her cheeks puffed up from the drugs she was taking, and I kicked over the driftwood and searched through clumps of grass at the edge of the dunes. As she vomited and withdrew from eating and, I feared, living, I trudged along the shore line, back and forth from the rock pools to the open sands, wanting every wave to deliver me more. If I could get enough shells to fill the first twelve blocks of the wall, then Annie would get better enough to come home for her twelfth birthday.

We made it, Annie and I.

She came home and we ate birthday cake in the tiny courtyard behind the shop. She had on the bright red beanie that Mum had knitted for her and she picked at the crumbs of the cake and talked of how she wasn't really better but she was going to have a special transplant. She had a month to go to have tests and if they were all clear she could get stuff from her mother's bones and it would be put into her bones and if it worked it would make her completely better.

A month.

Twelve more sandstone blocks. I had to cover them all.

"If they won't let me visit you," I told Annie, "I'll take photos to show you how I'm going. Every weekend. We'll make it."

She squeezed my hand.

I lay awake till midnight. I crept downstairs and found the city bus map and I marked every beach. The next morning I went online and got the bus and train timetables and printed them off. Mum found me scribbling information on the stickers I had placed on each part of the map.

I shook my head when she asked what I was doing.

"Would this have something to do with Annie?"

"Maybe."

"And is it something to do with the shells you've been gathering each time you go off to the beach with Dad?"

I didn't say anything.

"Because maybe we understand more than you think. Maybe we could help you."

That's how they joined in when each weekend I said I wanted to go to the beach. We roamed further and further from the centre of the city. We went up the North Shore, to the tips of every peninsula. We found coves and inlets that were deserted. We went to tiny beaches at the edge of the National Parks and the three of us became fossickers. We gathered large shells and small ones, perfect shells and broken ones, beautiful shells and ordinary ones. And when we returned, we laid them, almost touching, along the top of the sandstone wall. Then we took another photo for Annie's mum to take in and stick up above Annie's bed.

Today is going to be our last trip. Annie's tests two weeks ago were fine and she's back in intensive care, getting ready for the transplant tomorrow. There is one block of the wall to go. We're driving further than we've been before, down the South Coast. Mum says there's a beach past Kiama that's seven miles long. She says we'll walk the lot of it if necessary. Two coffee jars are what we have to fill. Mum worked out that a jar and a half is what we need, but we'll get some more, just to be sure. We'll be back by dinnertime and we'll lay them down and they'll cover the whole wall. Then I'll ring the nurse on Annie's ward and get her to pass on the news and our good luck when she goes in for the operation.

She's going to be fine.

Make Friends, Make Friends, Never Never Break Friends

JULIA GREEN

The whole thing about best friends is that you tell them everything, isn't it?

Lauren and I have been friends forever. Our mums met each other when they were pregnant with us. From almost the moment we were born (only twelve hours apart, but on different days, because I was born just after midnight), we were spending time together. We have the photos to prove it. I've got two propped up against the mirror in my bedroom. One was taken when we were six weeks old, lying on a cream blanket. Lauren's the baby with blonde wispy hair and a white lacy cardigan (hand-knitted by her gran) and I'm the other baby: dark hair, turquoise Babygro. We're holding hands. In the other one we're about two. It's summer, in the garden. Lauren's pouring water from a little plastic teapot over my head, looking very serious because she's concentrating, and I'm laughing. Her hair's in little bunches, and mine's a bit straggly (because of the water).

We went to toddler group together, and nursery, and started reception at infant school the same day. Mrs Evans put us on the same table, and Lauren's drawer was just along from mine.

When we were a bit older, on the days Lauren's mum worked, Lauren came home with me, and on the days my mum worked, I went to her house. We liked the same food (pasta bake), the same TV programmes, the same games. I've got this really vivid memory of us in the playground, seven years old, chanting this rhyme along with all the other girls, and knowing that Lauren and I really meant it: *Make friends, make friends, never never break friends.*

We told each other everything. Sometimes we even knew what the other was thinking. We'd meet up in the morning to walk to school, and find we were wearing the same clothes (pink gloves, purple tights, new black patent shoes).

When we were eleven, Mrs Marshall chose Lauren to be Annie in the school musical and I only got a part in the chorus. I was upset at first and things were a bit awkward for me and Lauren, but we got over it. And it didn't matter when she started being so good at maths, because I was better than her at English and art. There was one brief, horrible time when a new girl, Justine, came to our school, and tried to be best friends with Lauren, giving her presents and inviting her back after school, but it didn't last long.

"Cam's my best friend," Lauren told Justine. "You'll have to be friends with both of us or not at all."

"Joined at the hip, you two," Dad said about Lauren and me. "Do you ever do anything apart?" He laughed. "You're like an old married couple!"

"Hardly," Mum said. "Name one married couple you know like that!"

Dad looked startled. "It's just a turn of phrase," he said.

The long, hot summer we were both thirteen, in our last year at middle school, Lauren and I spent most lunchtimes on the school field, lying on the dry grass and staring up at the blue, blue sky, seeing what shapes the clouds made (cat, dolphin, hippo) and talking about *everything*. As the days crept towards the end of term, everything seemed to be tinged with a mix of sadness and excitement. Everyone in our class would be going to new schools in September. Different schools, depending on where we lived. We'd be right at the bottom again, instead of the top, like now. Our lives were about to change forever.

One lunchtime in July, Lauren and I lay on the grass and discussed our lists of which boys in our class we fancied. Neither of us was surprised that we had the same top three: Ryan, Marek, Jake. Ryan was gorgeous, we both agreed. It was funny: we'd known him since we were about five, but he seemed different now, somehow. When had the change happened? It had been so gradual, perhaps, we'd hardly noticed.

"Would you go out with Ryan, if he asked?" Lauren said.

"He won't ask. But I might, if he did. Would you?"

Lauren laughed. "Only if you didn't mind. *Do* you?"

I looked at her pink face. "He's already asked you, hasn't he?"

She turned her face away, slightly, blushing even more, and I knew she'd already said yes. It was the first time, I think, that she'd had a secret from me. I wondered when she'd been alone with Ryan, and he'd asked her. Right in the pit of my stomach there was an ache I'd never felt before.

When we went back into class for the afternoon I watched Ryan, and watched Lauren, but there was nothing different I could see. We were writing in our English transition books (the books we would take with us to the senior school). Lauren's story was about a girl who discovers that the people she thought were her parents aren't really. Her real parents are rich and famous and on an exploration mission somewhere. It was good.

I couldn't think what to write.

Going out with a boy didn't mean you actually *went* anywhere. At least, I didn't think it did. Lauren and I still walked home from school together that afternoon.

"You're quiet," Lauren said. "What's up?"

"Nothing."

"You don't mind about Ryan, do you?"

"Of course not."

"Good," Lauren said. "It doesn't make any difference to us, Cam."

It was so hot that the tarmac felt sticky on the soles of our sandals. We stopped off at the shop to get ice pops. Lauren paid. We walked down the Avenue, in the shade of the lime trees. Lauren seemed to be going slower and slower.

"It's Friday, remember? I've got my riding lesson at four-thirty," I said. "Hurry up."

Lauren looked at her watch (brand new, expensive, from her gran: ready for the new school). "You've only got fifteen minutes. You'd better run on ahead. You don't want to be late."

She was dawdling on purpose. It suddenly dawned on me *(duh!)*: she was waiting for Ryan to catch up. But I didn't say anything. I just went on by myself. It was the first time I'd ever done that.

I thought about it at bedtime. Everything was changing. End of one thing, beginning of another. That was OK. That was how it was supposed to be. But I'd expected Lauren and me to stay the same. Forever. I felt silly, now.

Her being friends with Ryan shouldn't have made any difference to me, but it did. When Lauren phoned in the morning, like she always did on Saturdays, before we went up to the stables together, I knew I sounded a bit off.

"Guess what?" Lauren's voice was all excited.

"What?"

"Guess!"

"How can I?"

She sighed. "It's about you."

"What, then?"

"You and Marek!"

That aching feeling came again. "And?"

"He wants to know if you'll say yes if he asks you out. Ryan told me."

I stared at the phone.

28

"Well? Go on, say yes, then we can all be together, you and Marek and me and Ryan. You said you liked him, before, didn't you?"

"I don't know," I said. "I don't think I want to go out with anyone."

I heard a soft sort of sigh, as if Lauren was really exasperated with me.

"Shall we meet up, anyway?" I said. "Like usual? You and me."

"But I said we'd go to town and meet Ryan and Marek!"

She'd already arranged it! I felt furious. "Mum doesn't like me just hanging round town," I said. "I'm going up to the stables, like usual."

"Please, Cam."

"No," I said. I felt horrible.

"Why not? It will be fun. Come on, don't be like this!"

"Like what?"

"Moody and jealous."

"I'm NOT jealous!"

"Yes you are. You're jealous of me and Ryan!"

"I am so not! I don't want to go to town, that's all. Or out with Marek."

Lauren made an exaggerated sighing sound. Then, in this icy tone, she said, "Time to grow up, Cam! Get a life!"

I couldn't believe it! My best friend, saying that! I stared at my mobile, and then I pressed the end call button. It was our first real argument. I felt like crying. But I was cross, too.

I went up to the stables by myself. Everyone noticed, of course. "No Lauren today?" "Is she OK?" "Never seen you two apart!"

After I'd mucked out Hatty's stall (Hatty is my favourite horse, a beautiful bay mare with a star on her forehead) and brought her back in, I stroked her nose and lay my head against her warm flank. She felt warm and comforting. She nuzzled my hand, searching for titbits, and blew warm air down her nostrils. It wasn't the same without Lauren there, but I'd rather be with Hatty and the other horses, out in the sunshine and fresh air, than hanging round shops in the stuffy town centre any day.

Usually we muck out one stable each, and that means we can have a free ride, so someone else had to do Charlie's stable that week. I didn't take much notice who, until I got back from my ride across Rough Common. A boy. Older than me. Dark hair. Deep brown eyes. He smiled. I smiled back. My tummy did a funny fizzing thing.

My mobile bleeped: a message from Lauren. *Missing U. Sorry 4 earlier.*

I texted her back. *Me 2. C U L8r?*

She came round at about three. We went out into the back garden.

"You didn't miss much," she said. "All we did was hang around the precinct, and eat chips, and then the boys went off to see some crusty movie at the Odeon. *Bor-ing!*"

We were lying in the sun, on the same cream blanket that's in the baby photo, though it's worn and tatty now. Lauren lay on her tummy, picking at daisies in the grass. Her hair looked golden and shiny, like a shampoo ad, and her skin was this amazing colour too, smooth and beautiful. No wonder Ryan liked her, I thought. She looked older than me now: not twelve hours, more like twelve months, or more.

"How was Charlie?" she said.

"Missed you," I said.

She laughed. "Really? How could you tell?"

"Just the look in his eyes. Big and sorrowful. And the way he flicked his tail. But someone else mucked out his stable and rode him, so he was fine, really."

"Good. I think I'm going to give up riding. There won't be time, not this summer, with us going away, and once school starts in September everything will be different."

I thought of the new boy at the stables, the one with dark hair and dark eyes, who'd ridden Charlie and mucked out his stable, but for some reason I didn't say a word to Lauren about him.

I suppose that's how it starts. First one little secret, then another. Bit by bit, they build up, like bricks in a wall.

We were going to be apart over the summer holidays, Lauren and me, because her parents had taken the whole summer off and they were flying to America for the holiday of a lifetime (that was what Lauren's mum said, anyway). They'd start in New York, visiting Lauren's auntie, and then hire a car and go all over the country, east to west coast. "I'll send you postcards from every place we stay," Lauren promised. It would be the longest we'd ever been apart. Six weeks!

"How will you manage?" Dad asked me. We had our two-week camping holiday in Cornwall to look forward to, but the rest of the time Dad and Mum would be working.

"I'll be fine," I said.

"It'll do you good," Mum said.

I frowned at her. "What do you mean?"

"Well, you can spread your wings a bit. Be yourself. It isn't always easy, being part of a *pair* all the time. Being in someone's shadow."

Dad gave Mum a funny look.

"I'm *not* in Lauren's shadow!" I said.

"No? But you've been friends such a long time. And now you're both growing up, and changing… things will be different, Cam."

I started going up to the stables more often. The horses needed exercising and I liked helping with the lessons for younger children. Sometimes the boy was there, sometimes not. I found out his name was Asim. He was shy. He didn't talk much. But he smiled a lot, and I smiled back. He looked quite a bit older than me, I realised. More like fourteen – fifteen, even. He was brilliant at riding. I watched him sometimes, the way he handled the horses. He whispered in their ears, and they'd do anything.

The first postcard arrived from Lauren. *New York's AMAZING! Cool shops. Miss you. xxx* I pinned it on the board in my bedroom next to the mirror. By the end of the summer, the board would be full.

It rained solidly for our first three days in Cornwall. I was actually glad Lauren hadn't come on holiday with us; she'd have been miserable. She so hates being cold and wet! And in a tent… well! We spent most of the time in cafés and pubs and all the things-to-do-on-holiday places which were under cover: art gallery, local museum, marine aquarium, indoor swimming pool. Lauren would've hated all that, too. *I* was miserable, to begin with, but then on day four the rain cleared, the sun came out and the sea turned from slate grey with white bits to brilliant beautiful turquoise, and I learned to surf! *That* was amazing! Mum and I took lessons every morning for the next five days, and by the end we could both do it. Dad was dead proud of us. He took action photos with his new digital camera. Even I had to admit I looked fit in a wetsuit!

I wrote Lauren a postcard, even though she wouldn't get it till she came back from America at the end of August. *Surfing – better even than galloping full pelt across Rough Common! Missing you. xxx*

"*Missing you*," I wrote, because that's what we always said, but the truth was, I wasn't, really. I was having a brilliant time, and Lauren was a thousand miles away across the Atlantic! That was new. I even joined in with this crowd of kids on the campsite who played stuff like frisbee and football every evening. We were all different ages, about six to sixteen, boys and girls, and no one cared and it was friendly and easy and fun. Mum and Dad went off for walks and to the pub and did stuff together, without me, for once. Sometimes it's hard work being an only child. You feel *responsible*, somehow, for making your parents happy.

So I was sad when the holiday was over. And a bit scared about what was going to happen next, i.e. school. And glad I had Lauren to go with. I was looking forward to telling her about my summer, too.

We hadn't seen each other for six whole weeks then. My pinboard was full of her postcards, except for the middle, where I'd pinned the photo of me surfing, and one of all of us kids at the campsite, larking about.

She didn't get back till the day before the new term started. We spoke briefly on the phone (she was tired from the flight) and arranged to meet, to get the school bus together.

Mum and Dad waved me off. Dad took a photo – me in my new uniform. "You look so grown up!" he said.

"You've grown about a foot over this summer!" Mum laughed. "And it suits you, that wind-blown surfing look! Have fun. See you this afternoon."

I had a shock when I first saw Lauren, waiting at the end of her road. It was partly the green blazer and short black skirt, and her hair, which she'd had straightened, and her face: pale, with dark eyes: jet lag? or (surely not!) makeup? But there was something more than that, too.

"Hi Cam!" she said. "Wow! You look, like, really different?"

I hugged her, and she felt different too. Not like Lauren, my best friend, at all. "Did you miss me, then?" she asked.

I didn't tell her the truth, of course. I sidestepped. "Thanks for the postcards," I said. "Was it amazing? The US of A?"

"Guess so." She wasn't convincing. Poor Lauren. Perhaps it hadn't been the holiday of a lifetime after all.

Even her voice sounded different. Sort of American, a bit fake. "How was yours? In Cornwall?" she asked me, and it struck me how awkward we were being with each other. Like strangers, almost.

"Brilliant," I said. "I learned to surf, and made loads of friends, and I really want to go back there next year, or half-term even."

Lauren looked at me in this weird way, as if she didn't want to hear any of it, about my good time. As if she'd much rather have heard I'd been miserable, and lonely, and missing her. I felt suddenly sad. That wasn't how best friends were supposed to be, was it?

We arrived at the bus stop. Asim was in the queue. My tummy did the usual loop-the-loop.

He smiled. "Hello, Cam."

Lauren spun round and gave me such a look. "Who's *that*?" she demanded. "How do you know *him*?"

I felt my cheeks go hot. "Asim," I said. "He rides, sometimes."

"You never said before. What's going on?"

"Nothing," I said. "What's the matter with you?"

She flounced round. "You never used to have secrets."

She started talking about her holiday, then, showing off. "America," she said, "was life-changing! Awesome." It was the sort of thing her mum might have said. It didn't ring true. "Of course, you wouldn't understand," she said. "You can't, since you've never been anywhere abroad, have you?"

I stopped listening after a while. I was remembering what Mum had said about people changing. Moving on. I supposed that was what was happening to me and Lauren. And it felt OK, I suddenly realised. Not the end of the world after all.

The bus pulled up. We piled on. "Upstairs or down?" I said.

"Up, of course!"

I wished we hadn't, once we got up the stairs, with the bus lurching all over the place. It was really crowded. There was just one spare seat.

Lauren hesitated. She looked at me.

"No standing upstairs!" the driver yelled.

"You sit here," I said. "I'll go back down. I don't mind." And I really didn't. I stumbled downstairs to the lower deck.

At the back of the bus, someone familiar patted an empty seat. He smiled at me.

"Thanks," I said, relieved to sit down. And happy, too, that it was next to him.

"Nice that you're coming to our school," Asim said. "I missed you at the stables. How was your holiday?"

So I told him. He listened. And that was how I started making my new best friend.

It was never the same with Lauren after that. We're still friends, of course; we probably always will be. We've a whole childhood we share, after all. Photos. Memories. But things changed that summer, forever, and that's fine. We grew up. We grew different. That's how it is, sometimes, with best friends.

Toad Crossing

FRANCES THOMAS

The first time I saw Tiggy Jones, I really didn't like her; not at all. She had this little white squashed witchy face and short black hair which stood up in spikes. When she looked at you, she screwed up her bright black eyes and peered disconcertingly close to your face. (This was because she needed glasses, which they gave her a year or so later – she was fine after that.) Her Welsh accent ran up and down the scale like a clutch of mad violins. And what a stupid name. It was short for "Tegwen", which was like no name I had ever heard before. The person I really wanted for a friend was Brenda Simon, a doctor's daughter, with an angel-pure face and fat butterscotch plaits that hung halfway down her back. I longed for her to notice me, but she wouldn't. She swanned around with her gang – Dilys, Babs and Valerie – like a princess.

It was the second year of the war, and I'd been evacuated, sent to stay with the Bensons, just over the Welsh border. They were nice enough – an elderly, careful couple. But it wasn't my home. My father was away in the army, and to me, being in the army meant getting killed. And, if the bombing made London so dangerous that I couldn't be there, what about my mother, who'd stayed on? I felt ill with fear and homesickness.

The Bensons lived in a detached villa just outside town. I remember the fat crimson three-piece suite that no one ever sat on, the bathroom that smelt of icy water, and the slippery pink eiderdown in my bedroom. I was polite, obedient, and because I was so unhappy, not very friendly. I think they were disappointed in me, but they never said, of course. In those days, people never said much about how they felt. They put a brave face on, and struggled away. Things are different nowadays, and better I think, though sometimes I'm startled by the way people express their feelings all the time. But it means they're less likely to be unhappy in the ways I was unhappy in 1941.

I went to the girls' grammar school in town. They wore a maroon uniform – pleated tunics, white shirts, striped ties, and big black hats called "velours" with maroon-and-green hatbands. Because I'd just started school in London the term before I was sent away, I wore my London uniform – the same hideous assembly, but in navy blue. I'd liked my school in London. And I'd made some friends too; I wanted to write to them but I didn't like to ask the Bensons for writing paper. When my mother wrote, once a week, she enclosed a stamped addressed envelope with a blank sheet of paper inside for my return letter. That way we wouldn't "impose".

I didn't like the new school. I don't know why – I just didn't. Probably it was having to start all over again with all the new-school things. I fell behind in everything, and no one bothered to help me catch up.

I said Brenda Simon didn't take any notice of me. Well, she didn't, for a long time.

Then she did.

These days people discuss bullying – you can talk to teachers, or ring helplines. I'm not sure that stops it happening; I think some people will always be bullies if they can get away with it, but at least maybe the people they bully know they aren't alone. I felt that no one else in the world had ever been through what I was going through. And I thought that somehow, something I was or did made me deserve it.

It started off almost unnoticeably. I'd be walking down the corridor, and then suddenly I'd be aware of a rustling behind me. I'd turn suddenly, to find Brenda and her gang frozen and suppressing giggles, as if they'd been playing Grandmother's Footsteps. Some days my velour hat would go missing, and I'd find it on somebody else's peg in the senior cloakroom. Splashes of ink would appear over my exercise books. The cruellest thing they did was to leave newspaper cuttings inside my desk, with photographs of people being bombed in London. Once, they'd drawn in a little house amid the smoke, and written "Elizabeth's House". I knew it was them because of the giggles and whispering, and I tried to confront them.

"Look," I said, waving the latest cutting. "This just isn't funny."

They giggled and clamoured in unison, *"This just isn't funny!"*

"I know it's you doing it!"

"I know it's you doing it!"

"You won't get away with it!"

But all they did was to repeat my words – and anyway, what could I do?

One Saturday afternoon, I was mooching around the Bensons' house. I sat in my room for a bit, came downstairs, picked up a magazine. I was bored rigid. But this made nice Mrs Benson uneasy, and I knew that if I hung around, she'd find things for me to do that I wanted to do even less.

42

So I put my coat on and said, "Is it all right if I go and play with my friends?"

Mrs Benson looked relieved. "Of course it is, duckie. Off you go," she said. (Being called "duckie" was one of the things I didn't like about being with the Bensons.)

So I was out of the house at least, though of course there *were* no friends and there was nowhere to go. There was a big lake in the town, with a café and benches to sit on, dating from the days when it had been a fashionable holiday resort. Without any idea of what I was doing, I wandered off in that direction, expecting to sit on a park bench, looking at ducks for the next two hours.

When I checked the time on the clock over the café, I found I'd only been out for fifteen minutes. I didn't know what I was going to do.

It would take maybe another fifteen minutes to walk right round the lake – it was a large lake. At the far end, there was a wooded area, which marked the edge of the town. There was real countryside beyond – farms and animals. A few elderly couples were also doing the walk, and here and there a man was fishing. But by the time I reached the path by the woods there was nobody else around. Or so I thought.

I came across her suddenly, crouched in the

mud in her gaberdine school mac. She looked up at me, squinted, and when she saw who it was, gave her mad little grin.

"Hello, Elizabeth," she said.

"Hello, Tiggy," I replied, my heart sinking. In addition to being bored, I'd just confronted the class weirdo. But she was scrabbling away so intently, I forgot my awkwardness, and crouched down beside her. "Tiggy, what in heaven's name are you doing?"

"I'm looking for toads." Toads? Did the girl have a broomstick hidden away too?

"Whatever for?"

She raised herself up and looked up at me. "Because the toads live here…" She waved at the woods. "And they breed *there*." She pointed at the lake. "They cross the road in the night and the early morning. The school bus goes up and back, and the Hereford bus, and Mr Evans's car, and usually Morris's tractor. In the morning, you see dozens of dead toads. It's really sad. I'm just helping them cross, so they don't get squashed. Want to help?"

It was the longest speech I'd ever heard from her, and one of the most sensible I'd heard from anyone in my class. Tiggy had noticed a problem, and was just getting on with sorting it.

Still, I wasn't sure about picking up a toad. I'd hardly ever handled a live animal in London, except next door's kittens once. Tiggy scrabbled around in the mud. "Look, here's one," she said.

It was really horrible – brown and warty with blinky dark eyes. When she held it up, it kind of flopped in her hands as though it was filled with liquid. "Ugh," I said.

I thought she'd tease, but she didn't. "People think they're slimy," she said gently. "But they're not. Look, if I put it in your hands, you can take it across the road, then it'll be safe."

"Won't it come back?"

"Not till it's done its business. Go on. It won't hurt."

Partly lulled by her encouraging voice, and partly not wanting to seem cowardly, I took the thing. She was right. It wasn't slimy, but dry and cool. And it didn't make any sudden movements. By the time I'd taken it across the road, and laid it gently in the reeds that fringed the lake, I wasn't frightened of it anymore. Only then did Tiggy give her witchy cackle. "Bet you didn't think you could do that, London-girl," she said. But it wasn't said nastily, the way Brenda and her crowd would have said it.

For the next couple of hours, we scrabbled in

the mud looking for toads and helping them across the road. We'd helped a couple of dozen, but Tiggy said there'd be hundreds. I realised with a shock that it was getting dark. The time had raced by and I hadn't noticed. "I've got to go," I said reluctantly. "Me too," said Tiggy. "But we can carry on tomorrow." Then she said, "Oh, Elizabeth, I do think even toads deserve justice, don't you?"

With anyone else you'd have laughed, or got embarrassed. But when Tiggy said this, I found myself agreeing with her.

From that moment, I had a friend. Tiggy was funny, kind, and much smarter than she'd seemed at first. One day I went home with her. She said, "The only thing is, you have to promise not to fall in love with my brother Gareth." I thought this was an odd thing to say until I saw her brother; he was quite astonishingly good looking. At seventeen, he seemed far too old for me, so I didn't fall for him, just felt horribly shy in his presence. Brenda, apparently, had a crush on him; meeting Gareth was the one thing that could turn her into a soppy mess. In spite of his looks, he was a gentle, obliging young man. "He'll do anything for you, that lad," said Tiggy's mother, who was a larger version of Tiggy, complete with mad giggle. She baked wonderful cakes – with everything rationed,

I hadn't tasted food like hers for years. And I loved their muddy, untidy farm, with the milking shed by the stream, and the sheep chomping away at the emerald grass. I was still desperately homesick, and worried, of course, but having Tiggy as my friend took the edge off.

Brenda, though, continued to persecute me. And she was getting meaner and nastier. I wondered where it would end. "She wants teaching a lesson, that one," said Tiggy, clutching my arm. But in the class hierarchy, Tiggy simply wasn't important enough to sway Brenda. "We'll get her, girl, somehow, I promise," she said one day when I'd opened my desk to find a dead mouse. I didn't see how she could.

Girls had to do an awful lot of needlework in those days, and very tedious it was. We were blanket-stitching cot sheets for bombed-out babies one day, and to while away the boredom, the teacher read to us as we sewed. It was a book of fairy stories, which we were all too old for and had heard before. There was the one about the princess who has to kiss a horrible frog before it turns into a prince. I never trusted that story. If he could change once, he was quite capable of changing back. Suppose the princess were to marry him, only to find he'd preferred being a frog after all? Best stick to a prince without amphibian connections, I thought.

But the story had fired something in Tiggy. At lunchtime, she got all excited as we sat in a corner of the playground. "Listen," she said, "I've thought of a way to get back at Madam Brenda. It'll be complicated. But I reckon we can do it."

It was complicated. It was daft. Only Tiggy could have dreamed it up. Plus it needed the cooperation of Gareth. Tiggy was sure she could manage that. "He hates bullies," she said confidently. "He'll help."

On Wednesday evenings, Brenda and I stayed at school late. We had been signed up by our mothers for an elocution class, my mother because she thought it would make me less shy, and Brenda's mother because she wanted to eradicate all trace of a Welsh accent from her daughter's voice. Our journeys home coincided for part of the way. There was a bus shelter surrounded by trees where I would turn right while Brenda went on. On these journeys, she would pretend to ignore me, but then turn round and hiss something really spiteful at my face, such as, "Your mother's really common, London-girl! She eats like a pig, doesn't she? Oink, oink!" It was stupid, but usually by the time I reached the Bensons' front gate, there'd be tears in my eyes.

But this Wednesday, as we left the school together, I felt different and a little unreal. I couldn't believe that what we'd planned was going to happen. I couldn't believe that I was going to do it. I wanted it not to be happening, but at the same time, I was excited that it was. Things couldn't get any worse for me than they were, so whatever the outcome, it had to be an improvement.

But it depended on me getting it right. And it depended on other things happening in the proper sequence. Could we really carry this off?

Brenda observed how ugly my freckles were, and then bounced ahead. That was fine. I knew something – somebody – would be waiting out of sight behind the empty bus shelter. My heart was pounding. I must act fast, before Brenda turned the corner and was gone.

I found what I was looking for – a box – and carefully lifted something out of it.

Then I called Brenda. She stopped in her tracks, surprised, for usually I never addressed her first. She saw me holding something. I had to make my voice sound confident and cool. "Hey, Brenda, look what I've found."

She came forward, saw what I held and said, "Ugh!"

By now I was still scared, but I had also found a

strange, intoxicating confidence and I carried on. "Bet you don't know what it is."

"Ugh! It's a hideous frog!"

"It's actually a toad. But a very special toad."

She stared at me, unable to believe my temerity.

"Remember that story Miss Elliot told us? If you kiss it, it'll turn into a handsome prince and walk home with you."

"Oh yes?" she sneered.

"But you wouldn't dare kiss it, would you?"

"Are you mad? Are you completely crazy?"

"Because if you won't kiss it, I will," I said. "And then you'll see."

I'm not saying this is something that would work against all bullies. I didn't even know if it was going to work against this one. I certainly wouldn't recommend anyone to try it. But I did. Or I pretended to. I pretended to kiss the toad.

Brenda gave a loud cry of disgust, and flounced off. "You are so stupid! Well I hope you die of poison! I hope you die!"

For a few seconds, nothing seemed to happen. I was caught like a spider in a web, trapped in those empty seconds.

And then, suddenly, he was there.

"That's not a nice thing to say, Brenda," said a quiet voice, my handsome prince, Gareth Jones.

He'd slipped out so quietly from behind the shelter that it seemed he really had appeared by magic. For the briefest of moments, even I believed he might have done. I felt as exhilarated as any magic princess might feel who was caught in a delightful spell.

And he gave me a lovely smile. "I've come to walk you home, Elizabeth. Just as I promised."

Brenda had stopped in her tracks at the sound of his voice. She turned, slowly – reluctantly, almost. Her mouth opened, then shut. She turned pale, then she went red. She'd been caught out behaving like a pig, and in front of someone she admired, too. You could almost read the thoughts flashing over her face – surprise, confusion, disbelief. And humiliation. Oh yes, humiliation. That was the best thing.

I don't suppose for one moment she really believed I'd turned a toad into Gareth Jones. (If she'd looked carefully, she'd have seen that I was still clutching the toad – later we released it by the lake.) But she wasn't quite sure what had happened, except that she'd been wrong-footed, and outsmarted. She'd been ganged up against in the way that she and her friends had ganged up against me – and she didn't like it, not one bit.

After that, though she never became friendly –

and after that, I never wanted her for a friend – the nastiness stopped. School became better, though I was still homesick.

I don't know how long I stayed with the Bensons. It seemed like forever. But one day, Mum turned up with a suitcase. "Please let me come home with you," I begged. "I don't care about the bombs." So I went back to London, and though, like all wartime children, I had some narrow escapes, I got through the war safely enough. So did my mother. And so eventually did my father.

Tiggy and I stayed in touch. After the war, she came to visit us in London, and later on I went to visit her. I liked her even more as she grew older; she stayed funny, eccentric and brave. Later she became a music teacher, and the choirs she trained were always winning prizes. When I had children of my own, we often spent summer holidays with her. Gareth ran the family farm for years, until he retired, and now his son has it. Everyone thinks Gareth is a lovely old gentleman, but only us older ones remember how handsome he once was.

Sometimes Tiggy and I don't see each other for years, but when we get together, it's always as though we've never been apart. I'm a grandmother now, though my grandchildren assure me I'm "really cool" for a granny. They enjoy the story of

Tiggy and the toads. It always makes them laugh.

A few weeks ago, the phone rang, and there was Tiggy, with her mad Welsh cackle. "Come and see me again, girl!" she begged. "We might both be dead next year, who knows!" Though she sounded far from dead when she said it.

My car was out of order so I went down by train. Tiggy met me at the station, spiky white hair still standing up around her face, dangly earrings and a pink and purple top. After she'd clutched me with a delighted scream that stopped people in their tracks for miles around, we piled into her little car. "Now, I've got two things to show you before we get home."

"Nice things, I hope."

She laughed. "One is. The other... well... look."

As we drove down the High Street, we saw an elderly lady shuffling up the road. She was shapeless and badly dressed with wispy hair. She carried a stick, and we saw her poking it at a little dog which had approached her with a friendly wag of its tail. Her face was sour and scowling.

"Know who that is?"

"Haven't a clue."

"That's Madam Brenda. Turned out nice, hasn't she? She's living with her daughter now, but they can't stand each other. Want to stop and say hello?"

The thought made me shudder. "No thanks! Show me the other thing."

"Aha!" said Tiggy. "Now, this you'll like."

We drove through the town. It hadn't changed that much, though there was a supermarket now, and a pizza restaurant, and some new houses beyond the library.

"This is the way to the lake, isn't it?" I said, as we turned into a road between trees. She stopped the car with a screech of brakes. "Look there!" I looked. There was a road sign, a red warning triangle. In the triangle, a picture of a toad.

"That's the Toad Crossing," she said triumphantly. "And every year now, the council closes this road in the breeding season so the toads can cross safely. Took us years of campaigning, and hundreds of dead toads, but we did it, girl, we did it!"

For a moment, I glimpsed my old school friend, with her black hair and her school mac, crouching in the mud.

"Justice for toads at last," I said. "Well done." She looked at me quizzically. I don't suppose she remembered ever saying that, but I remembered.

Justice for toads, justice for people. It doesn't always work out that way, and sometimes it can take a long, long time, but it's great when it does, don't you think?

Under the Influence

Marcia Byalick

Some things just don't happen. Planes don't crash into your house. You don't get struck by lightning. And your best friend in life doesn't publicly, shockingly, horrendously dump you for no reason.

The middle school cafeteria smelled of French fries and damp sweaters. As always during lunchtime, it was crowded and loud.

"So Ali, I think I changed my mind," Emma began. "I think I'm going to get a labradoodle instead of a golden retriever."

This must be the fifth time she changed her mind. No one but me knew she meant when she graduated from college and we lived together in New York City. Our shorthand conversations were a habit that came with being best friends since third grade. Whether we talked about our soon-to-appear breasts or our almost-always-annoying mothers or our probably-never-going-to-happen boyfriends, it was clear we were not only on the same page, we occupied the same sentence.

"Fine," I dismissed her, "but first we really have

to decide what to do with our lockers."

After reading the suggestions in this month's *Teen Vogue*, we narrowed the choice of decorating the inside of our locker doors to either putting up postcards of the places we wanted to visit one day, or hanging up pictures of people we admire.

"I'm thinking collage... John Lennon, Madonna, Lance Armstrong, Tina Turner..."

"Cool, then I'll do the postcards."

Just like that. Done deal. Life had to be so much harder without a great best friend. I smiled, remembering Emma's emails each summer when I went to sleep-away camp. *Come home. Why aren't you home?* And when I got home, we'd pick up right where we left off.

Emma gulped her cranberry juice. This was our second week of drinking cranberry juice in little glass bottles with our lunch. We were the only ones in our class who did and it was Emma's idea to see if we could start a fad. Not that too many of the things we liked ever made it to anybody's top ten list. We both chose to wear our clothes in a medium rather than a small, not because the small didn't fit, but because the mediums were more comfortable. We loved the old black-and-white TV shows more than we liked MTV. Each of us had a horoscope calendar, sure there was definitely something mystical about how often they were right. And maybe because we were both only children, each of us had a memory wall in our bedroom filled with pictures, most of them of the two of us laughing till our faces turned beetroot red.

Suddenly there was a loud squeal from the table behind us. I rolled my eyes even before turning around to see exactly which drama queen needed her fix of centre stage. The girls who sat there *said* they were friends, but they weren't the nutritious kind like Emma and me. When you were one of the half-dozen or so who were welcome to have lunch there, it signified your membership in the tribe... the tribe of those who worship Geena.

If you called them the popular girls, they'd deny it, saying there was no such thing – but you had to be popular to believe that. I want to say they were just not as nice as the rest of us but then it's so confusing. How can you be popular if most people don't like you?

"It was so easy," Zoe said with a small smile, relishing the response as the photo on her mobile phone made its way around the table. "Yesterday Kim was in the locker room, changing for volleyball practice. When I saw she was wearing knickers with the days of the week on them, I couldn't resist. I mean, WEDNESDAY, in pink letters, like we wore in kindergarten! She was completely oblivious – never even saw me standing there."

I felt a force like a tornado building inside me. Kim was a new girl in school. She had really short, dirty-blonde hair, really long arms, and the awkward, stretched-out features of a girl who was about to explode and grow six inches in the next month. Whatever she did to deserve such a punishment, I was sure she didn't have a clue.

"Next time she'll think twice before she pushes ahead of us in the lunch queue," Zoe proclaimed, sipping her diet Snapple.

"You should see your face," whispered Emma. "I don't care if you hate them, stop staring."

She was right. This wasn't my battle. So why did it bother me so much?

Then it happened. Geena's eyes locked onto mine. I felt caught in her sight, like a fly on sticky paper. I had no choice but to eyeball her right back. That she in all her lemony vanilla beauty tried to stare me down didn't bother me. I wasn't afraid of her like the rest of them.

To this day I don't know how she did it, but without moving a muscle, she went from looking right at me to looking right past me. Then she turned to Zoe and smiled silently. In unison they turned back to me with the best impression of a deadly ninja stare that girls who owned pumpkin-coloured mobile phones decorated with Hello Kitty stickers could muster.

Thank God, the bell rang. I watched as Geena stood up first, the rest of them orbiting around her as they moved towards the hallway. Suddenly the whole platoon stopped short, right in front of us. Geena glanced down at the remnants on my lunch tray. She picked up the empty wrapper from a small bag of Doritos that Emma and I had shared.

"Should you really be eating those?" she asked, her melon-coloured glossed lips parting in a big smile. The girls behind her didn't move. Each one of the seven tiny jewelled tank tops agreed that the thinner you are, the better you are. Full stop.

"Should you really care what I'm eating?" I answered in my most intimidating voice. My face felt hot.

"Don't be that way. I'm just trying to help." She dismissed me and turned to Emma. "Is that a new shirt? I love it. I have sneakers that would look so hot with it."

"Thanks," stuttered Emma. "I love your hair clip."

I wanted to kill Emma.

Then the whole world changed forever. Geena unfastened her hair clip and handed it to Emma.

"Here, take it. I have two. It'll look really pretty on you."

My heart did a back flip.

"Thanks," Emma repeated. "That's so nice of you."

As Geena, the sun, moved away, her planets trailed in her shadow. When she reached the door she turned and riveted her eyes on me. Her half-smile was a sneer in disguise.

"Just watch who you give the evil eye to," she said quietly. Although she stood some distance away, I heard every word.

I stuck out my chin, ignoring my wildly beating heart. Then I turned back to Emma, just in time to catch her grinning at herself in the mirror, her hair adorned with her new pink rhinestone heart.

"You never liked Geena. You told me terrible things about her. Remember how you made fun of her T-shirts… each one was worse than the last."

I was talking to Emma later that night at our regularly scheduled wrap-up of the day. "Remember, in one week she wore, *Not all stars were made equal, You're ugly and that's sad* and *Seriously. Old people have got to go.* Come on, you gagged too, admit it."

There was silence on the other end of the phone.

"Oh please, even if you don't say anything, it's still true that you thought she was awful."

"If you're just going to go on about Geena, I'd rather finish my maths homework. I get it. You don't like her. Do I have to hate her because you do?"

I didn't exactly hate Geena. But I did hate the idea that Emma was defending her.

"Are you finished? Can I hang up now?" Emma pleaded. "I'm tired of this conversation."

"Sure, be that way," I said, finally letting her off the hook. "I'll see you tomorrow."

I wasn't exactly sure what happened that day but I knew whatever it was wasn't going to improve my life one bit.

When I got to our table at lunchtime the next day, Emma wasn't there. I sat down and took out my lunch. The noise from the next table drowned out my growling stomach.

"Do you like my hair this way?"

"Anybody have a pair of tweezers?"

"Does this jacket make me look humongous?"

Then I heard the world's most familiar laugh. I turned to see Emma sitting on the same stool as Geena. At that instant, our eyes met. I felt strangely calm, almost cold.

"Hi," Emma said, popping out of her seat as if

someone had lit a fire under her bottom. She rushed over to me, but her book bag stayed under Geena's seat.

I quickly turned back to my sandwich but not before catching Geena's smile. In that split second, I understood. I was being punished for having the guts to stare her down. How stupid to think there was nothing she could do to me. Now we were in a fight without having one, with Emma, my best friend, as the victor's prize.

I noticed it was the first time Emma was wearing the shoes we'd bought together the previous Saturday. I had to stop myself from telling her how good they looked.

"We'll talk later, OK?" I said, trying to hide my devastation. "No worries."

Emma nodded.

I gathered my things and walked away, focusing intently on the red exit sign.

"Cool shoes!" I heard Geena squeal as Emma returned to her half of the seat.

"You may as well get used to it, honey. That's the way girls are," my father said, his mouth full of broccoli. "Am I right, Sue?"

"Well," my mother said, "I could understand if it were the other way around. I mean, you're the gutsy one, the risk-taker… you…"

"I would never in a million years move to that table and leave Emma. Never," I answered, much louder than necessary.

It wasn't my parents' fault. I couldn't tell them the part about Emma being used to pay me back for having an eye-duel that told Geena I wasn't afraid of her. Although I'd bet my entire shell collection it was true, I knew how ridiculous it would sound if I said it out loud.

"I seriously doubt Emma's not going to be your friend because she sat a few feet away from you at lunch today," my father said kindly. "Why don't you call her? I'll bet she feels worse than you do."

Of course she did. That made more sense than that my life was over. I ran to my bedroom to call.

The phone rang an uncharacteristic three times before Emma picked up.

"Hi there," I said, careful to sound perfectly normal. "What's going on?"

"Oh Ali, I'm so glad you called," Emma bubbled. "I was so scared you were mad at me."

Flushed with relief I was about to reply when she continued, "But I'm on the other line. Can I call you right back?"

I'd rather have plucked my eyelashes out than ask who she was talking to.

"Sure, whenever," I answered breezily. "Later."

My heart raced while I waited for Emma's call. Suddenly I was afraid. What if she decided being friends with me ruined her chances of being popular? What could I say? "You have a choice, them or me?" Is that the way a real friend treats someone?

The phone interrupted my thoughts.

"OK, let's talk," she began. "You are my best friend in life. Nothing can change that. But I can't lie to you… I really, really like sitting at that table. And I swear, Geena is not the wicked witch you think she is."

I just listened.

"If you give me a few days, I'm sure I can get you to sit with us," she pleaded. "Say yes, please…"

Us? She was part of *us* and I wasn't? That was quick. One three-dollar hair clip versus six years of secrets and giggles and hugs and tears.

I thought of how having a best friend like Emma always made me feel safe, like I was twelve feet tall and bulletproof. What now?

"I don't ever want to sit there…"

"Just think about it, OK?" she interrupted.

It was the first time in history she hadn't a clue what I was feeling.

I had no practice at being angry at Emma. So when I saw her opening her locker the next morning, I just had to make things better.

"Hey," I mumbled, "don't be angry."

Emma looked at me, then turned back to her locker.

"I'm not angry," she said hesitantly. "We can't expect to agree on everything all the time. I shouldn't have asked you to sit with us. You're right, it's not your thing."

"No, no, I'm glad you asked. And I'm glad you understand why I can't."

"Can't?" Her voice suddenly grew louder. "I don't understand why you *can't*... I just know you *won't*. There's a difference." She slammed her locker and picked up her books. "Look, it's fine, OK?"

It so wasn't fine, but I didn't answer. What would I say? I could only shut up and accept that a friendship in trouble is better than a friendship that's ended.

A few days later Geena stopped me in the hall.

"Emma and I were talking last night about how stupid all those Harry Potter films were," Geena said pleasantly.

Emma and I had gone to see each one together, and the Emma I knew loved every single one.

Then she inhaled deeply and said, "Promise you

won't take this the wrong way, but I never understood how you and Emma were such close friends."

I wasn't sure where she was going with this.

"I mean, I like her… a lot… but she's not as mature as you are."

My toes curled in my sneakers.

"Look," Geena continued, "I want you to sit with us at lunchtime. It's hard to find a girl who couldn't care less if someone else disagrees with her." Then she looked right into my eyes and said, "There are only a few of us, you know. We should really stick together."

A few of us? Us, meaning her and me? I felt like I was in an alternate universe.

"Just promise you'll think it over, that maybe you might be wrong about me."

When the history of the world is written, I'm sure that this day in my life will not be in it. But it felt like it should be.

"I'm so glad you and Geena bonded this afternoon," Emma gurgled that night. "I knew you'd like her if you got to know her."

"How do you know I bonded with Geena?" My heart quickened.

"She just emailed all the girls about how great you are."

I realised I was clenching my teeth.

It made me think of my grandma's advice: if you're not sure a pair of shoes fits, it doesn't. Unfortunately, that doesn't always mean you don't buy them anyway.

When Geena saw me approaching the table, she stood up. "Omigod, sit here," she said, indicating the other half of her tiny stool. She raised her chin up and to the left, directing Zoe to vacate it and move to a seat across the table. Emma smiled proudly.

On the floor under her seat were Zoe's maths book and science workbook. Geena's name was written in bubble letters all over them. In all the years Emma was my best friend, I never once thought to write her name on my stuff. That's what fans do.

I watched and listened as if I were in a foreign land, which in a way I was. If one of those teen magazine fashion patrols came along, I'd be the yuck at the end of the yeah, yeah, yeahs. Sitting up close, I noticed the multi-coloured beads around their necks and the dozen slim shiny bangles on their wrists, all coordinated with the layering... tank top under T-shirt under short zip-up jacket. Their skin smelled vaguely fruity, like their hair that swayed every time they turned their head. I was overwhelmed with what went into getting ready for school each day. I felt like their plain, blotchy-faced little sister.

Emma was wearing camouflage combat trousers and an orange pleather wristband. In her ears were these fishing bait earrings. If I didn't know better, I'd think someone dressed her while she was sleeping. It was hard watching her savour every forkful of Geena's friendliness.

Gone were her fake Uggs... and the plaited friendship bracelet I made her at camp last summer. I wondered if she still listened to Simon and Garfunkel or admitted loving Judy Blume or watching The Simpsons, or whether it wasn't cool to like them anymore. She was sitting right across from me, but I missed her.

Then, without warning, Geena said, "So, Ali, word is you still suck your thumb."

My mouth dried up. How could Emma tell them that? I felt naked in a room full of people, with no one to hand me a blanket.

"I did too..." she continued, "until I was four."

Everyone laughed. I never felt so tricked. My heart pounded in my ears. I stopped myself from finding Emma's face, afraid the naked rage behind my eyes would cut through the air between us like a knife.

"Do you believe everything you hear?" I heard myself answer through clenched teeth.

A dozen embarrassing stories about Emma popped into my mind. The way she uses a tape measure across her chest every month and marks down the progress. How she wishes she could go to sleep-away camp with me each summer but she's afraid she'd miss her parents. How she can't fall asleep without the light on.

"Speaking of habits that are hard to give up," I blurted out, "did you hear that Emma still collects American Girl dolls?"

Everybody stopped talking. Then I turned to Emma. "How many do you have now, nine? Or is it ten?"

"Very funny," Emma said, her face tightening like a fist.

"More true than funny, don't you think?" I persisted. I couldn't believe how much I hated this new version of my best friend.

Emma glared, then turned her back. I would have preferred her to hit me.

"Lighten up, Ali," Geena smiled. "Being honest is not the same as being mean. It was just a joke."

In that instant, I realised how easy it is to make someone feel bad. You don't have to actually be smarter or prettier or thinner or funnier than they are, you just have to make them believe you are. You have to get them to see themselves in your mirror, like they have in the funhouse at the fair, which distorts how everyone really appears.

That night was the first time I was ever nervous to hear from Emma. It would be horrible if she didn't call, but what would she say if she did? The phone rang right on time.

"Hey, what's going on?" she began. Then before I could reply, she added, "Look, let's just forget what happened, OK? It was stupid."

First off, it wasn't stupid, it was mean. Second, she sounded way too casual. Emma just wanted to shut down a fight before it began. While she didn't want to lose my friendship, she didn't want to admit she started it either.

Then something happened that had never happened before. We had nothing to say to each other. I couldn't reveal anything I didn't want Geena to know. Suddenly, I understood that while my Emma still existed, she was buried inside one of those girls who sat at that table. And she wasn't about to jeopardise her seat... for anything.

"You know I can't sit there anymore, right?" I said softly.

"I know, Ali," Emma sighed. "I understand."

My eyes filled. In those five words, I heard my old Emma, only now she was saying goodbye to us.

The light next to my computer shone directly on the memory wall of photos behind me. There we were, Emma and me, splashing around at the beach, dressed as the queen of hearts and the queen of spades for Halloween, in front of my house on our way into New York City to see our first Broadway show. It was hard to think about those times. And impossible to believe they were over.

I learned as seventh grade wound down that the further away you are from the centre of popularity – in my case, Geena – the harder it becomes for the powers that be to hurt you. Their real heat is reserved for their own. From my vantage point across the cafeteria, I learned that the benefits of hopping off the popularity treadmill included eating peanut butter sandwiches and wearing friendly trousers that don't give you wedgies. And the last thing I learned as the year came to a close is that if you smile whenever someone makes you cross, instead of telling that person how you really feel, all those angry feelings can build up and poison you.

If this were a fairy tale, I'd tell you that Geena finally got what she deserved, and that I found a new friend who's even better than Emma. But this is real life, and none of that happened.

I'm happy at my table, where no one rates my outfit or judges how my hair looks. Recently, Emma waved to me across the cafeteria. Maybe it has something to do with her mother calling my mom to ask for information about sleep-away camp.

Maybe I'm just being optimistic, but I know that girl. I figure it's just a matter of time before she screws up the courage to walk over.

T4J

Sophie McKenzie

I slumped in the chair, my head in my hands. *Not again.*

It was Monday evening. Homework time. Except I'd left my thicko-spellers-group homework at school.

I groaned out loud.

It wasn't really called the thicko-spellers group. Its proper name was the Year Seven English Language Support Group.

Whatever. It basically meant you were rubbish at spelling. Apparently, I was good at reading comprehensions and even better at making up stories. But I was so bad at spelling the words inside them, Mrs Dickenson said she needed a special Tyler-to-English dictionary to understand what I'd written.

Very funny. Not.

I slumped further into my chair.

Tonight's homework was "spelling sentences" – where you're given a list of words and have to put each one into a sentence. Mrs Dickenson says that using the words in a realistic way helps you remember how to spell them.

You're supposed to learn the spellings off by heart first. But if you don't bother with that bit, it's really quite easy.

I thought through my options.

Forgetting the whole thing was the most tempting. But all that would happen then was detention, and having to do the homework anyway.

Maybe I could break into school, commando-style, and steal the list of spelling words from my desk. A cool idea. But sadly impractical.

Or I could phone one of my friends from the thicko-spellers group and get the words off them.

Mmm. A no-brainer really. But who to call?

There were three other people in the group. Tom was the obvious choice. I'd called him before about homework. And we were good mates, usually. But we'd fallen out today over this stupid gang Tom had set up. Tom's Top Crew, he called it. The T.T.C. He wouldn't let me join. I mean, like who made him the boss of anything? So I couldn't call Tom tonight. No way.

Naz was the other boy in the group. But he'd been away from school today.

Which left Jessica.

Jessica was organised. She was bound to know

the homework. And we got on well. We were friends, even. Well, friendly, at least. Yes, she was the perfect choice. Except… Just one problem. One massive, awesome, insurmountable problem.

Jessica was a girl.

If Tom knew I'd called Jessica, I'd never hear the end of it. On the other hand, I had to call someone. And surely *Jessica* wouldn't say anything?

Before I could think about it anymore, I gritted my teeth and dialled her number from the class list on the notice board. I'd make the call quick and to the point. Like a commando on a mission. Retrieve the information and retreat.

The phone rang.

A girl answered. "Hi."

"Jessica?"

"I'm her sister."

"Oh." *Stay on target.* "Hi, is Jessica there?"

Silence.

"Who's calling?" Jessica's sister sounded like she was trying not to laugh.

On target, mate. Retrieve and retreat.

"It's Tyler." I paused. "Tyler from school." I could feel my cheeks getting hot. That was a stupid thing to say. I mean, how many Tylers could Jessica know?

"Hang on." Jessica's sister smothered a giggle.

"Boy for you, Jess," she yelled.

I winced as the sound of footsteps turned into muffled giggling.

Retrieve and retreat, mate.

"Hello?" Jessica's voice at last.

"Hi." I was so wound up after talking with her sister, my words came out in a rush. "Jess, it's me, Tyler. I left my spelling book at school and I need to know the words we're making sentences with."

Silence. "OK." She hesitated. "Just wait a minute."

I could hear voices in the background, but I couldn't make out what they were saying.

Then Jessica was back. "So where'd you leave your spelling book?"

"In my desk, I guess." I shrugged. Why did it matter where it was? It wasn't here with me now. That was the point.

"So, you really left it at school?"

I rolled my eyes. Why on earth did she think I was phoning her? "D'you have the words?" I said, pointedly.

"Sure." Jessica cleared her throat. "They're all inanimate nouns, whatever that means. Technology. Democracy. Discography."

"Stop. Slow down." My pen hovered over my paper. "You have to spell them out. Yeah?

It's spelling homework."

Jessica started again, spelling the words out slowly. When she got to "discography", she stopped. "What does that mean?"

"It means all the music someone's recorded," I said.

"Nothing to do with discos, then?" Jessica giggled.

"No." I frowned. Why couldn't she just get on with the list? Getting the words was only the first step. I had to think up some stupid sentences to put them in next. And the United game was live on Sky at 7.30.

"Are you going to the school disco on Friday?" Jessica said casually.

"Er…" What did that have to do with the homework? "Dunno. Er… maybe. I guess so."

Silence. I glanced at the clock. The match started in twenty minutes. "Um… thanks for your help…"

"That's OK." Jessica paused. "I'm going too."

Going where? I gripped the phone more tightly, not enjoying the way the conversation seemed to be reeling wildly away from me.

Retrieve and retreat, mate.

"Are there any more words?"

"Er… yeah." Jessica spelled them out.

I thanked her again and hung up. Then I raced

through my sentences in time to catch the whole of the United game.

Sorted.

It took all of five minutes for me to realise there was something wrong at school the next day. I was rummaging in my desk for my United collector cards, when Tom sauntered over.

"Hey, Tyler." He grinned at me. "I hear you've been getting help with your homework."

I glared at him. "What are you talking about?" I knew full well, of course. Somehow he knew I'd called Jessica. Why couldn't she have kept her mouth shut?

Tom's grin deepened. "So did she agree to help you with anything else? You know. Anything *other* than homework?"

I looked round. Quite a few of the guys in Tom's new T. T.C. gang were watching us. Several girls too.

"You are such a jerk," I hissed. "I had to call her. I forgot my spelling words."

"Yeah, right," Tom smirked. "Why didn't you call me?"

I shrugged. I didn't want to get into the whole business of Tom's stupid gang and why I hadn't wanted to phone him.

"I just knew Jessica would…"

"Oo-ooh, Jess-ic-a." Tom said her name all slow and sarky. Most of the people watching us laughed admiringly. Tom didn't take any notice. That's typical Tom. Always acting laidback – like he doesn't care what anybody thinks of him, good or bad.

My face reddened. I bent over my desk. "Whatever."

I was trying to make out I didn't care either, but inside I was burning up with humiliation. Why had I called Jessica? I should have known Tom would find out. Better to have left the homework and done the detention.

"Hi, Tyler."

I jumped.

Jessica had somehow crept up without me noticing. She was smiling shyly, all big, brown eyes and long, dark lashes. I didn't smile back. In fact I wanted to yell at her. Freakin' bigmouth. What was she doing, blabbing about me phoning her to everyone?

"Look, he's all embarrassed," Tom sniggered.

"Thanks for calling last night, Tyler." Jessica blushed, then she put her hand on the edge of my open desk, right next to mine.

Tom laughed, but I hardly heard him. I was staring, transfixed, at the back of Jessica's hand. The writing was tiny – too small for the others to see – but it was clear. Clear to me, anyway.

Three letters. Printed in blue ink across the base of her little finger. *T 4 J.*

Oh no. *T 4 J. Tyler 4 Jessica.* Is that what she thought? That I *liked* her?

My chest tightened. *Please. No. This couldn't be happening.* I started closing my desk lid.

Jessica moved her hand away and flicked back her long, brown hair. "So I thought about it, and the answer's yes – I guess I could go to the school disco with you." She was speaking quietly, but loud enough for everyone within a metre of the desk to hear.

Wolf whistles and cat calls started up all around us. Led by Tom.

I blinked. *What?*

"I… er… I…" I knew my face was bright red now.

"See you later." Jessica slipped away.

"Ha! Tyler's got a girlfriend." I looked up. Tom was turning to some of the other girls in the class who had wandered over, clearly intrigued by all the noise. He started explaining loudly what had just happened.

My heart was in my shoes. How on earth could Jessica have thought I wanted to go to the disco with her?

More importantly, how was I going to tell her I didn't?

The day went from bad to worse. I could tell people were whispering about me behind my back wherever I went. Then at lunch break I walked past a group of Jessica's friends in the cafeteria queue. They started chanting:

Tyler and Jessica sitting in a tree
K-I-S-S-I-N-G!

I was out of there faster than a speeding football off a United striker's boot.

I avoided Jessica for the rest of the day. I had no idea what to say to her anyway. The whole thing was just too embarrassing. I considered talking to Mum about it. But I knew she'd only ask all sorts of impossible questions about how Jessica had sounded and how I'd felt.

Maybe Dad was a better bet. I hadn't seen him at the weekend, so I knew he'd call tonight to make some arrangement for Wednesday after school.

When he did, we chatted about last night's game for a bit. Then I swallowed. "Er... Dad?"

"Yeah?"

"I was just wondering. If someone you know has got the wrong end of the stick about something, what's the best way to tell them?"

"Mmm." I could picture Dad's face screwed up in a frown. "What sort of someone?"

I hesitated. "A friend." I blushed. Thank goodness I was on the phone, so Dad couldn't see my face.

"I see." Dad paused. "Er... girl or boy?"

Ouch. "Er... girl actually," I said, as casually as I could.

"I see," Dad said again. "And how d'you know she's got the wrong end of this stick?"

"Because she thinks I asked her to go somewhere with her and I didn't," I blurted out. "I definitely didn't. But she wants to go anyway."

"Right." Dad chortled down the line. "Ha! Good on yer, son."

What? "No, Dad. I didn't ask her. We're just friends."

"Sure." I could tell Dad was grinning now. "Sounds like she wants to be more than friends."

That floored me. My heart raced. *No.* Was that it? Jessica *liked* me? *Me?*

I thought about it. It made sense. It sort of explained the *T 4 J* on her hand. And yet...

"Why didn't she just say what she meant?" I said. "You know, ask me straight out if I wanted to go out with her?"

Dad laughed. "Welcome to the weird and

wonderful world of women, Ty. If you figure it out, let me know."

The next few days passed in a blur. I avoided Jessica as much as I could, but it wasn't easy. Especially when we had to go to the thicko-spellers support group on Thursday morning and Tom made a big show of me sitting next to her. At least she'd scrubbed that *T 4 J* off her hand.

You'd think it would feel good, someone liking you. I mean, Jessica was nice. Pretty, even – she had all that long, silky dark hair, and a little nose that turned up at the end. But I didn't fancy her. I really didn't.

No way.

Like I'd said to Dad. We were just friends.

On Thursday after school, Tom and I played football in the park with some of our mates. Afterwards Tom gathered the guys from his gang together. I ignored them and headed for the exit on my own. I heard footsteps pounding behind me and turned round. Tom ran up.

"Hey, Tyler. D'you wanna go to a T.T.C. meeting at my place tomorrow night?" He paused, then made a silly face. "No, wait. You're going to the stupid school disco, aren't you, with your *girlfriend*."

I glared at him. "I already told you, she's not my…"

"Come to the gang meeting, then," Tom said. "It'll be better than a boring disco. Look, I was only kidding about you not joining. Yeah?"

My heart leapt. *Yes*. Then it sank. If I didn't go to the disco, what was I going to say to Jessica? I mean, she was sort of counting on me now. It would be mean if I didn't show up.

Never mind, I'd sort that later.

"Sure," I said casually. "No problem."

"Good." Tom ran off.

I went home, determined that first thing tomorrow I would find a way to tell Jessica I wasn't going to the disco.

I got to school early the next day, then waited outside our classroom until I saw her walking down the corridor. She was alone, thankfully.

This was it. Retrieve and retreat. Retreat.

"Hi," I said. "About tonight…"

"I know." Jessica fumbled distractedly with her bag. "I thought it'd be best if you came to my house to pick me up before the disco. Is that OK?"

What? I stared at her. *No*.

She smiled at me – a hopeful smile that made two tiny dimples in her cheeks. Funny. I'd never noticed those dimples before. They were kind of cute.

Get a grip, Tyler.

I didn't want to go to the disco with her. I didn't want to go to the disco at all.

I wanted to go to the gang meeting.

"Cool," I heard myself saying. "What time should I come round?"

"About quarter to seven." Jessica's dimples deepened. "Thanks." She disappeared into the classroom.

I leaned against the wall and closed my eyes.

Fabulous, Tyler.

Absolutely fabulous.

I turned up late at Jessica's. It was gone seven, the time that the disco was due to begin, and the light was fading. She opened the door, her jacket already on over her jeans, her face pale.

"God, I thought you weren't coming," she gasped. "Let's go, before my sister comes down."

I shoved my hands in my pockets. "Look," I said firmly.

"Bye, Mum." She slammed the door shut and grabbed my arm, running away, half-dragging me along the pavement.

As we reached the corner, she slowed down and let go of my arm. I stopped, my heart pounding. The wind was cold, whipping across my face. This was really it now. We'd be at the school in five minutes if I didn't say something.

"Jess? Listen."

She looked up at me. Her eyes were all round and anxious – a soft, deep brown. I swallowed. This was way, way harder than I'd expected. If I told her I didn't want to go to the disco, I might really hurt her feelings.

"What?" Jessica said impatiently. "It's already started. Come on."

"Maybe we shouldn't arrive together," I stammered.

She stared at me. "What?"

I took a deep breath. "I just… I mean… it's like, we don't want people getting the wrong impression… "

Jessica frowned. "Don't talk rubbish," she said. "We're just walking in together."

I stared at her. "But…"

"Look, Tyler, I'm sorry if I've been a bit weird about this, but I thought you'd understand. I mean, you've always been a mate and I didn't plan… "

"Wait. Stop." *What on earth was she talking about now*? "In English, please."

Jessica sighed. "I know everyone's been teasing you all week, but that was sort of the point."

I stared at her, completely bewildered. "*What* was the point? What was the point of *what*?"

"I… I wanted people to think you were into me." Jessica blushed. "But it's OK, I know you're not."

She didn't sound very upset. I frowned. I mean, I didn't really care, but after worrying about her feelings all week, it was a little annoying to discover she didn't have any.

"Look," Jessica went on. "All you have to do is talk to me for a bit when we arrive. And maybe a dance or two. That's not so hard, is it?"

I shook my head. "If you didn't… I mean…" I sighed. "Why did you make out you wanted to go to the disco with me then?"

"OK." Jessica bit her lip. "If I tell you, do you promise you won't tell anyone?"

I nodded.

"Promise?" Jessica repeated. "As in a total and perfect act of friendship?"

I rolled my eyes. *For goodness' sake.* "Yes, I promise."

"It's Tom," she said. "I wanted him to ask me, but he didn't, so when you rang, I thought maybe if he thought you and I were going together, it would make him jealous."

I stared at her. She wanted to make Tom jealous? *That* was why she pretended to fancy me? That was why she'd been making out to everyone all week that I fancied her. Making me look stupid.

Anger surged up through my chest as I remembered the writing on her hand. *T 4 J.*

Of course. Tom. Not Tyler. *Tom 4 Jessica.*

That was what she really wanted.

"That was nice of you," I said, sarcastically. "Making me look like a jerk all week. Nice. A total and perfect act of friendship, in fact."

Jessica looked down at the pavement. Her hair fell across her face. "I'm sorry," she said.

There was a long pause.

She didn't fancy me. I blinked, taking it in. You'd think I'd feel relieved, but...

Jessica looked up. Her eyes glistened with tears. "I'm sorry, Tyler. I didn't think about it like that. I'm really... "

"Forget it," I snapped. "Anyway, you're wasting your time. Tom isn't even going to the stupid disco. He's having a gang meeting at his house." I took a step away from her. "In fact, as you obviously don't really want me here, I think I'll go and meet him right now."

I took another step away. "See you at school next week, yeah?"

Jessica's face crumpled. She turned away.

I stared at her. Panic filled me as tears trickled down her cheeks. Part of me, most of me, wanted to walk away. But something was stopping me.

"He doesn't even know I exist," Jessica wept.

Fear whirled through my mind, paralysing me. This commando voice was shrieking *retreat, retreat* in my head. But my feet were stuck to the pavement.

"I've tried all these ways to make him notice me, and none of them have worked," Jessica sobbed. She took a deep breath and wiped her eyes. Then she looked up at me, clearly making a big effort not to cry anymore. "It's OK, Tyler. You get off. I'll be fine."

This was my chance. *Retreat. Retreat.*

Right.

I looked at her. "What are you going to do now?"

"Everyone's going to expect me to turn up at the disco with you." Jessica's lips trembled. "If you're not even there then I'll look really stupid. But it's OK, I'll be fine." She dissolved into tears again. "God, this is the worst day of my life. And look." She unzipped her jacket, revealing a little black top that just skimmed her stomach. "I even wore my lucky top," she said. "I got kissed in this last summer and *he* really liked me."

I wrinkled my nose. Too much information. And yet… I looked at Jessica's face. Even with wobbly lips and red eyes she was still, undeniably, pretty.

I thought how much I'd wanted to be in Tom's gang.

Then I looked at Jessica's face again.

Maybe spending the evening with a girl wasn't such a terrible idea after all. "D'you still want to go to the disco?"

Jessica looked up at me. "I thought you were going off to Tom's T.T.C. meeting?" she sniffed.

I shrugged. "I'm just saying, if you still want to go…"

"Really?" Jessica's eyes shone. "You don't mind?" Then she smiled – a huge, beautiful smile. "Oh, Tyler, I'm really sorry I made out you liked me. God, Tom's such an immature jerk compared to you. And… and I'll make sure this evening that everyone knows we're just friends, OK?"

"Whatever." I watched her zip up her jacket again. Who needed to be in a stupid gang, anyway?

"Maybe we should carry on pretending for a bit," I said. "About liking each other."

"You're a real friend." Jessica beamed at me. "You know, I'm actually glad everything's turned out like this."

I grinned back, then took a deep breath.

"We can even hold hands," I said. "If you want, that is."

"OK." Jessica slipped her hand into mine. It was small and soft.

It felt… well, it felt good.

We strolled up the road together. Jessica started chatting about the thicko-spellers group and how she hated being the only girl in it.

I didn't say much. Just listened, holding her hand, as the commando voice faded to silence.

Retreat?

I don't think so, mate.

I don't think so.

The Gardener's Daughter

JAMILA GAVIN

Shalini sat on the veranda, languidly rocking herself in the swing lounger, the earphones of her iPod plugged into her ears. She was listening to her favourite music.

It was the peak of the afternoon, and sleepily warm. Even the birds in the garden had gone quiet. Great Aunt was taking her usual nap inside the bungalow, but would appear in an hour full of liveliness and fun, and then they would DO something! "What shall we DO, Shanu!" she would cry, but she was never short of options to keep her young English niece amused: go for a bike ride, take a rickshaw into the bazaar, walk in the Dil Kusha gardens, or sit near the old Hindu temple and watch the boatmen coming in from a day's fishing.

While she waited for Great Aunt to wake up, Shalini had been watching a little Indian squirrel bounding along the top of the wall. Suddenly, it changed direction, leapt away and sprang into the nearby tulip tree. The reason for its flight became apparent as from over the wall appeared a small face.

Two large shiny black eyes challenged her. *Are you going to shoo me away, or are you going to let me come closer?* they seemed to say. Shalini stared back, then gave a little grin. The face broke into a broad smile, and a young girl in a ragged frock, who looked barely more than seven years old, clambered to the top of the wall and jumped down into the garden.

The girl kept her distance, staying close to the wall in case she needed to make a quick getaway, but her eyes remained fixed on Shalini. She continued to smile, tipping her head to the side, the Indian way, as if to ask, "Have we an understanding? You don't mind that I have jumped over the wall into your aunt's garden?"

Shalini smiled back reassuringly, while tapping her foot to the rhythm of the song which was pulsating through her ears. The child frowned, looking puzzled. She tipped the palms of her hands upwards and raised her shoulders. "What's that?" was her clear question.

Shalini beckoned her. "Want to listen?" she cried. She took the earphones out of her ears and held them out to the girl. The girl looked around, briefly unsure whether she should, then with a shy smile ran over to the veranda.

"Here, sit!" Shalini patted a space on the lounger next to her. She held up the earphones and demonstrated how to put them into her ears, then gave her the iPod. The girl plugged in the earpieces. She gave a cry of amazed delight and an enormous grin spread across her face. She jigged up and down and tapped her feet, twisting her arms as if she would break out into a dance.

After a while, Shalini indicated that they could each have an earphone, so that they could both listen at the same time. And it was thus that they were sitting, side by side on the lounger, listening to the music, when a motorcycle rickshaw whined its way to a stop outside, and Cousin Padma appeared at the gate with Kunti, her eldest daughter, who was Shalini's age.

Cousin Padma lifted off the iron ring, the gate swung open, and they walked through. She waved a superior hand at the child sitting next to Shalini, like a queen waves at a servant, indicating that she should shut the gate. The child immediately gave her earphone back to Shalini, and bounded over to the gate to do as she was told.

"Dirty little creature," declared Cousin Padma. "You shouldn't be so familiar with such children.

You'll pick up nits, or something worse. And I really don't advise you to flaunt your western gadgets around. It's not safe. These people are like monkeys, they'll have it off you before you can say 'Jack Robinson'." By the time Cousin Padma and Kunti had reached the steps of the veranda, the child had shut the gate and slipped back over the wall.

"Aunty's still asleep," said Shalini.

"Well, she'll be awake soon. I'll go and get Ranjit to make us tea."

That dashed it, thought Shalini; they wouldn't go off and DO something now. Cousin Padma would want tea and attention.

"Would you like to listen to my iPod?" Shalini asked Kunti.

Kunti's face brightened. "Oh yes! I've seen them advertised on television. Please let me listen."

"Absolutely not!" exclaimed Cousin Padma, returning from the kitchen, and pushing her away. "Those things have been in the ears of that dirty creature. You could catch anything. I suggest you go immediately and wash them with disinfectant before you put them in your ears again," she advised Shalini, forcibly.

Shalini sighed and put them away. She moved over to sit on a rickety cane chair nearby, allowing Cousin Padma and Kunti to occupy the lounger.

Shalini's heart had sunk at the arrival of Cousin Padma. She was her great aunt's eldest niece, who lived on the other side of town with her husband and their three children — two of them under seven, and the third, Kunti, who was nearly Shalini's age; a silent girl, cowed into obedience; hardly speaking unless she was spoken to, then only replying monosyllabically.

In the past, Shalini had stayed at Cousin Padma's house, though she had never enjoyed it. Padma was so bossy. She even bossed her husband around, and he seemed to do what he was told as much as the children. She never simply asked him or her children for anything, but always ordered them, as if they were her servants. So this time, Shalini was glad to be staying with Great Aunt during her holidays. Though elderly and widowed, she was full of mischievous fun. She always found Shalini something to DO, taking her out and about by day, and playing cards competitively, with huge bellows of laughter, each evening. But Shalini didn't like the way Cousin Padma seemed to be coming around so much, and how she had taken to bossing her elderly aunt around. She was beginning to behave as though she was mistress of the house.

Exactly when the hour of her nap was up, Great Aunt opened her door onto the veranda, her grey hair neatly brushed and swept back into a bun at the nape of her neck, her eyes glittering with wakefulness.

"Ah! Padma!" Aunty greeted her niece. "And you've brought Kunti. How nice. Now Shalini will have some company of her own age."

"You mustn't let Shalini play with those street children," Cousin Padma chided her. She'll catch something – and anyway, it gives them ideas."

"Ah! So the gardener's back for the season. How nice. It's only Uma, the gardener's daughter from next door," smiled Great Aunt. "She likes to pop over the wall and visit me when they come."

"I found her sitting on the lounger next to Shalini." Cousin Padma sounded outraged. "It's going too far. This isn't England. She shouldn't just make friends with any old riff-raff."

"It's all right," soothed Great Aunt. "She's a good girl, that Uma. I like her coming. I can get quite lonely, you know, and I enjoy having a child about the place. She's keen to dash about and do errands for me, and even Ranjit finds her useful."

"Huh!" Cousin Padma snorted, not in the least convinced.

"She's my little friend," murmured Great Aunt, as she cheerfully poured the tea and handed round the biscuits.

"Huh!" uttered Padma.

Shalini was just beginning to think that the afternoon was done for when, after an hour, and after they had each had a second cup of tea and a biscuit, Cousin Padma got to her feet and said, "Well, Aunty dear! Kunti and I have to go into town. We have an appointment with the tailor. We'd better be on our way. Shalini! Why don't you and Kunti go out and hail a rickshaw for me!"

As if she knew it was safe, Uma's face peered over the wall. "Does Ranjit need a hand with the vegetables?" she called in a high, pealing voice.

Great Aunt nodded. "Go see!" And Uma was off like an arrow.

The gardens Great Aunt referred to were her neighbour's gardens on the other side of the wall, belonging to a large, crumbling house left over from colonial days. The owners did their best to keep their property in good shape, and were able to employ a gardener for about three months of the winter season. Each year, he came with his wife and children. They would live in the servants' quarters nearby and, while he worked hard, tending the lawn, planting, pruning, seeding and making cuttings, his wife spent most of her time preparing their meals, washing their clothes, suckling her baby, and looking after her other infants. They were pleased that the eldest child, Uma, could earn a bit of money for the family by helping the old lady over the wall.

Every day, Uma climbed the wall to help "Aunty".

Ranjit, the cook, always seemed pleased to see the gardener's daughter, and accepted her offer to help with rolling out chapattis, sifting the rice, peeling the vegetables, picking out grit from the lentils and washing up dishes under the outdoor pump.

Yet really, it was the joy this child brought into the house that made Great Aunt's heart lift to see her. She was always singing, she skipped rather than walked, she laughed like a tinkling bell, and was endlessly willing to do anything that was asked of her.

In between tasks she and Shalini just seemed to get on. Shalini taught Uma some English, and enjoyed practising her Hindi with her. They both laughed together at nothing in particular.

"*Tu mera dost hai*," said Uma.

"I like you very much!" translated Shalini.

"I like you very much!" repeated Uma carefully, then burst out laughing. "Very much, very much!"

One day Uma didn't appear.

"I wonder where she is. They usually stay at least two months," murmured Great Aunt. Then

Ranjit told her. Uma's father, the gardener, had fallen ill, so the owners had paid them off and sent them away. Cook had seen the gardener, his wife and their troop of children, including Uma, with their bundles on their backs, trudging off down the road out of the city.

"Good thing too!" Cousin Padma muttered, when she heard Uma had gone.

Shalini was worried about them. "Where do they live?"

Ranjit shrugged. "They come in from a village outside the city. They'll be back next year – and if they aren't… well, there is always another gardener who will turn up at the gate."

Life became a little less bright after Uma left. Shalini knew that Great Aunt was anxious about the gardener, and missed the little girl. She missed Uma massaging her feet, and combing her hair, all full of chitchat like a little bird. If the truth be known, she felt as though Uma was the little daughter she'd always wished she'd had.

Some days later, a rickshaw turned up outside the gate. Shalini and Kunti had been swinging on the lounger. Kunti had Shalini's iPod plugged into her ears, while Shalini was reading. When Shalini heard a tinkling laugh, she looked up with surprised pleasure to see Uma getting down from the rickshaw, and thanking the rickshaw wallah for having brought her all the way across the city for nothing. The poor can show kindness to the poor – each knowing only too well how precarious life is.

As the girl skipped up the path with her laughing face, Cousin Padma stood on the veranda with her hands on her hips. "What do you want?" she questioned sharply.

"I thought Aunty might still need my help in the kitchen," said Uma, with unashamed charm.

"Oh yes, let her! Uma is very helpful!" exclaimed Shalini.

Padma glared at her English cousin in a "this is not your business" kind of way. "No. We don't need her." She waved Uma away. "We don't need you. The cook manages perfectly well."

"He was glad when I rolled out the chapattis. He said I did it perfectly." Uma presented her case with the skill of a lawyer. "He's always pleased when I sift the flour – and especially pick the grit from the lentils. He hates that job. He says my small fingers are just what's needed."

"We don't need you, I tell you! Now go home." Padma's voice rose. She had never liked the child. "She's too full of herself," she had remarked one day, noticing Uma leaning over one of Shalini's books when she was telling them all a story. She didn't find it proper for a servant girl to be so full of curiosity, energy and joy.

"But ma'am, I'm sure there are some jobs I can do. What about the washing or ironing? I can do it," persisted the gardener's girl.

"We have a *dhobi*, as you well know. There's nothing for you here. Now go."

At that moment, Great Aunt came out, having heard the interchange.

"Oh, Uma, it's you, is it? What are you doing here?" Her voice was kinder.

"My father is ill. I need a job," replied Uma eagerly. "I work well. I work hard. Please let me stay."

"She's just trying to scrounge from us," sneered Cousin Padma. "Send her away, Aunty."

"Let's ask the cook whether he would like her help, shall we?" said Great Aunt softly, and called, "Hey, Ranjit! Uma is back. She says you need her help. What do you think?"

Ranjit was an old man now. All that scrubbing of vegetables, kneading flour, sifting grain, and crouching over the stove made his back ache. He grinned a toothy grin, tipping his head from side to side, agreeing that she was a good little worker.

"Let her stay, then," murmured Great Aunt

gently, but authoritatively. "She can sleep in the kitchen."

"Huh!" snorted Padma. "You're a soft touch, Aunty. I don't trust her – all that smiling and charm. A little madam she is, if you ask me."

However, Uma stayed, and Shalini was so pleased. Once again, the house rang with laughter and mischief. The gardener's daughter seemed to cast spells; her gaiety was infectious. Even Kunti and her brothers fell under her spell when they came to visit. In between jobs she enticed them into games – got them running around, hiding, climbing trees, and getting grubby.

It had been arranged that Shalini should do some sightseeing. So one day, another aunt and uncle turned up to take her on a trip. They had booked sleepers on the overnight train to Delhi, and she would be staying with them for a month. They would go sightseeing to the Taj Mahal, and many other famous places.

"I'll be back soon," whispered Shalini, kissing her aunt goodbye. "I'll have another week with you before I go home to England."

She thought Great Aunt looked sad to see her go, and she comforted herself to think that Aunty had her little friend, Uma, to keep her company.

Shalini had only been away a month before she returned to Great Aunt's house, but there had been a drastic change. Cousin Padma had taken control.

"Aunty had a fall. She's getting frail now, and mustn't live alone anymore," Padma explained with… was it a note of triumph?

Shalini immediately noticed how dead the place seemed. When Cousin Padma's boys came round after school, instead of playing, they threw themselves in front of the television. Even Kunti went indoors, saying she must do her homework.

Uma had gone.

"Where is she?" asked Shalini.

"Oh, we sent her packing," exclaimed Padma. "One of my rings went missing. It had to be her. You can't trust these little brats. I warned you all, didn't I, Aunty?"

Shalini looked over to her great aunt. She was shocked. Aunty seemed smaller, crushed; as if in just a month, she had shrunk. She didn't answer but tipped her head sadly on one side and shrugged.

Shalini felt oppressed. She hardly dared to imagine what kind of life her dear great aunt would have from now on. Not only must she try to withstand her callous and overbearing niece, but she had lost Uma, her little friend, who had brought her such joy.

It was Shalini's last evening before going home. "Aunty, come! Let's DO something. Let's take a rickshaw to the Dil Kusha gardens," cried Shalini.

"Oh, what a good idea!" Great Aunt brightened, though in her heart she dreaded Shalini leaving her and going so far away. Who knew when she would see her again?

The shadows had lengthened like long fingers across the darkening green grass when they dismounted from the rickshaw and, with Great Aunt leaning heavily on a stick, they walked along the winding path towards an old abandoned tomb. The smell of flowers hung heavily in the air. As they approached the long flight of marble steps leading up to the tomb, suddenly a young girl came skipping down towards them. She held the lid of a cardboard box before her, looking for all the world like a little usherette selling ice creams in the cinema.

"Uma!" Shalini exclaimed with joy. "Aunt, look! It's Uma!"

"You buy? You buy?" Uma beamed up at them and held out her cardboard tray. It was not ice creams she was selling, but miniscule silver shoes, fit for fairy feet.

"How much?" asked Great Aunt, fingering them delicately, as if she handled pearls. They could see that Uma must have carefully collected silver wrappers from the street or the rubbish tip, wrappers dropped from sweets she would never eat. The shoes were so tiny, only a child's fingers could have fashioned them.

"As you like," her voice tinkled like a bell, "as you like."

Shalini bought two pairs, and Aunt bought one pair, but paid her enough for the whole tray. "Do you sell your shoes here every day?" she asked.

"Yes, ma'am. I'm here every day till sundown."

"Then I'll see you again," said Great Aunt, with a gentle smile.

They continued their walk, weaving among the flowerbeds. They could hear Uma's voice singing in the distance, "You buy?"

The next day, Shalini had packed all her things, ready for her journey home. She checked all around the house to make sure she hadn't left anything. She went into the bathroom, and her eye caught something glinting down the plughole. At first Shalini thought it was daylight, as the plughole led straight to the uncovered drain out in the road.

But it seemed to wink at her. She ran outside, curious to see what it was. There, lying in the gutter, partly covered in suds and roadside rubbish, was a ring. Cousin Padma's ring! Scooping it up, she raced back into the house to show her aunt. "Look!"

Great Aunt suddenly seemed to grow tall again. A glitter came back into her eyes. "Well!" she exclaimed, "I must DO something about this!"

On their way to the airport, Shalini looked across at the Dil Kusha gardens. She thought she saw a child dancing down the steps among the slanting shadows. She thought she heard a tinkling laugh. She looked up at her aunt and saw a faint but determined smile. She knew Uma would be coming back.

Speaking Esperanto

SHIRLEY KLOCK

If there's one thing I've learned about myself, it's that I need to eat on time. Otherwise, my system crashes, and I can't pay attention long enough to learn anything. Whenever I got in trouble at my old school, Mother always said, "Carma, you didn't eat lunch, did you?" I hated to admit it, but she was right.

I was really trying this year, but it was hard.

Not because I forgot. Because of them. The other kids.

And today, it looked like I was about to have a bad afternoon. I had just settled against the fence in my private corner of the school grounds when it began to rain. Cold water drizzled down the back of my neck, making me shiver.

The Winnie Krebs Day School had a perfectly good lunchroom. Everyone — everyone normal, that is — would be eating there right now.

On my first day, I'd gone there, too. I'd slid onto a bench alongside Elizabeth Warner, a serious-looking girl with long, dark hair. She bit the tip off a carrot stick, waved it at me, and said,

"Hi! You're Carmela, right?"

And, without thinking, I said, *"Saluton!"*

"What?" Elizabeth frowned. The word had just slipped out, a holdover from summer school. There, we ate by language tables, and I'd always sat with the other Esperantists. "Oh, sorry," I said. "That means 'hello'. In Esperanto."

"I've never heard of that," she said.

"It's this international language. It's supposed to help everyone understand one another. If we all learned it as a second language…" I stopped the explanation I had learned from my teacher when Elizabeth turned away.

"A *second* language? Weird," she said to the girl next to her, and they both laughed. Then, with one sideways glance at me, Elizabeth got on with eating her lunch.

OK, I was left out. I could deal with that. When I stood up to leave, I said, *"Ĝis,"* with a soft *"g"* which sounds sort of like "juice", only said fast. It means "goodbye". Elizabeth must have thought it meant something else because she looked shocked.

By the next day, if I went to sit with anyone, the other girls huddled up and turned their backs, like bees swarming. Their low voices buzzed with secrets. Sometimes they even moved away – the whole group of them – like I smelt bad. I actually sniffed at my lunch box. It smelled of pickles, that was all. Was that so awful?

And speaking in Esperanto? That hadn't helped. I guess Elizabeth thought I was showing off.

So I took myself and my sandwich and went to a far corner of the playing field. No one bothered me there. I could eat in peace. But I hadn't planned for a rainy day, and now, for the first time, it was beginning to rain.

"Please, just until I finish lunch? *Bonvolu*?" I asked the darkening sky. "*Esperanto*," I added. I thought of this word – it means "one who hopes" – as my own private abracadabra. But it didn't work this time. I gave up and ran inside, looking for a place to take cover. Not just from the rain, but from the other students.

I blamed my parents. It had been their idea to change schools. "You'll like it, Carma," my mother explained. "You won't get lost in the crowd. The teachers will have more time for you. And you can learn French!"

Winnie Krebs offered both French and Spanish. My old school didn't. This was all supposed to be good, but it made me nervous. Like a spotlight was on me.

I tried to explain that I didn't want to start again at a new school.

My parents insisted it was a done deal, that I would get used to it.

"You didn't want to go to summer school, either," said my mother. "And you loved it."

I'd been looking forward to getting back together with my friends at my old school.

"But I'm not so sure those kids are a good influence, Carmelita. Look how your grades have been on a downward trend. I want you to be with other students who are working hard." My father patted my arm.

I didn't want to be with hardworking students! I wanted to be with Kendra and Phillie; I'd known them forever. Most of the other new students at Winnie Krebs were boys. And the girls, who'd been together for years, were either cheerleader queens with polished fingernails or academic drones like Elizabeth whose shoulders were hunched from carrying too many books. They took one look at me and clustered into their own groups. I was left to hover outside.

I guess I looked different as well. Too different. My style was a cracked old leather bomber jacket – I loved it – combined with whatever my mother would buy me, usually tartan skirts and knee socks. At my old school, they were used to me and my style. But, at Winnie Krebs, they just thought I was strange.

Finally, I staged a major fit. "I just don't want to change schools!"

"I really think you'll benefit from the smaller setting. Look at this as an opportunity," my father said. In protest, I sawed off my hair with the pinking shears. It looked sort of moth-eaten, like I had parasites or something.

I pleaded with my mother. "I can't go to a new school looking like this!" But it hadn't worked. She'd sent me anyway.

Shaking off water droplets like a wet dog, I headed up the steps to the second floor. Maybe I could eat quickly inside the stationery cupboard. As I tiptoed past the art studio, Miss Devere stuck her head out. "I'm only… " I began, trying to think of an excuse for being in the hall without a pass, but she said, "Carmela! Are you looking for somewhere to eat lunch? My room is open."

I would never think anything catty about her tie-dyed skirts again. She held out one of the art smocks. "Here, I don't have any towels, but you can dry off with this. It's clean."

"*Dankon*," I said.

She smiled. "I'm guessing that means 'thank you'. And you're welcome."

I looked around the room. There were a few

other students at the tables. That's when I saw Pam. I knew her from our class, so I slid onto a stool next to her.

"*Saluton!*" I said. She looked nervous. I guess I hadn't made that great an impression on her, either.

The first week of school, our teacher, Mr Alpert, had started the Angel Network. It was a project to help the new students fit in. We drew names. The first assignment was to write a "positive note" to your secret friend. Pam was my assigned person. She wore soft grey and lilac and gold charm bracelets. If a teacher called on her in class, her pale face flushed and left a nervous rash. Awful. She was a wreck.

But I wrote her a note. It said, "I love your colours."

No one wrote me a note.

The next assignment was to Just Say Hello. You were supposed to say it to at least three people, including your assigned friend. This one boy, Sam, really got into it. He not only said hello, he made a banner with glitter letters and left it on his secret friend's desk. I saw him put it there, before school.

I tried to play the game the way Mr Alpert wanted. I said "*saluton*" to the first two kids I saw. And then I said it to Pam. She whispered, "Hi."

No one came up to me at all.

It went on like that until I was sure there'd been some kind of mistake. Somehow, my name hadn't been drawn. On the last day, your Angel was supposed to call you on the phone. Mr Alpert handed out a list with everyone's numbers. That night I waited and waited. No one called. Finally, I decided I wasn't going to call Pam, either. It was all just so fake.

The next day when Mr Alpert asked, "Did everyone enjoy their phone call?" I looked down at my desk. He paused a moment and then said, like he was surprised, "Did anyone NOT get a phone call?" No way was I going to raise my hand.

But Pam raised hers. Mr Alpert checked his list. "Carmela?"

"Well, no one called me, either," I said.

After school I had to meet with Mr Alpert, Pam and… no surprise, Elizabeth Warner. I loved Mr Alpert, with his longish hair and trim beard. He zipped around in his wheelchair with so much grace that you hardly noticed, and it also meant that he was on eye-level with us most of the time. I really wanted him to like me, even if no one else did.

But it didn't turn out that way.

When Mr Alpert asked Elizabeth and me why we hadn't made our calls, she just shrugged. "I don't know," she said. "It seemed kind of stupid. Not like real school. You don't get a grade on it, do you?"

"Would you have liked to get that call?" Mr A. asked me.

"I don't really care," I said, then added, "*Mi ne scias.*"

"Hmm?" He raised his eyebrows at me.

"It's Esperanto for 'I don't know'."

"Ah, interesting!" he said. "Maybe you can share some of what you *do* know with the class. Later."

When he turned to Pam, Elizabeth looked at me and mouthed, "Show-off!"

"Carmela did all the other things," Pam said. "It's OK." I didn't bother to point out that Elizabeth had done exactly none of the other secret assignments.

Mr Alpert sighed. "Try a little, can't you, Carmela?" and a chill breeze blew through me. I'd disappointed him. Elizabeth pelted out of the room, brushing against me on her way out.

"*Pardonu!*" I yelled, but Elizabeth didn't pause. "*Gis!*" I added. Pam turned to me, surprised. "It just means 'goodbye'," I told her. "*Esperanto,*" I added to myself. But there didn't seem to be much hope for me.

Finally, on that first rainy day, I found a safe hangout next to Pam in the art studio. Miss Devere

115

had a soft spot for us. Her own art was made of found objects left behind on the street, and I think she was aiming to add us to her collection. When I finally hitched myself onto a stool at a drawing table and looked around, I saw all the other fall-between-the-cracks kids. And now I was one of them.

The others were: a fat boy, Randall, who ate only low-fat plain yoghurt for lunch, Moselle, who, like me, spoke another language, only hers was her native tongue, and quiet Pam in her beautiful neat clothes. We misfits perched at the tilted drawing tables, not really talking to one another, just kind of doing parallel eating.

But then, something happened that changed my lunch strategy once again.

It was that snoozy time of the day, right after lunch, called D.I.R.T. – which sounds like it might even be interesting until you find out it stands for Directed Independent Reading Time. I saw Elizabeth pass a note. When Sue in the front row unfolded it, she turned around and looked right at me. I fingered my rough-cut hair. Maybe it was sticking up? It had been a huge mistake to cut it. I had to find a mirror.

But when I got to the lavatory, I didn't have a chance to see how I looked because someone was sobbing in one of the stalls, having a major meltdown. "Umm, *pardonu?*" I asked.

Immediately, whoever it was got quiet. Like the person had suddenly died in there. "*Pardonu me?*" I said even louder. "*Kion vi faras?*" (This translates as: Excuse me? What are you doing?)

"Is that you, Carmela?" blubbered a tiny, wet voice. A nose was blown. Used Kleenex thudded wetly to the floor. I examined the feet. Pink leather ballet slippers.

"Pam?" I said. "Are you OK?"

"I am dead," said Pam.

This was clearly untrue. "Can I come in? Or, can you come out?"

The door opened. Pam stood there, her face swollen, a rash blazing on her cheeks. "I can never come out. Not until *everyone* leaves."

"OK," I agreed. "Want me to bring you anything while you wait? Chocolate? A cushion?" She laughed and mopped at her face. Then she turned so I could see the back of her yellow capris. There was a rusty stain, a small one, really a very tiny spot, midway down her bottom.

"OK… " I said. "But, why the drama? It won't wash out?"

She turned on me. "Oh, who cares if it washes out!" I raised my eyebrows. "They'll see. And they'll know." She craned her head to examine her own backside.

"They'll know... what?" I said.

"That... I'm... having... my... period," said Pam, between clenched teeth. Her whole tone said, "You moron," but she was too polite to say the actual words.

But I got it. "Ohh, right," I said. It all became crystal clear. Of course. *The other girls* would never let her forget this.

"So, it's taken care of, though," I said, trying to get a grip on the essentials. She nodded, pointing at the metal box that dispensed pads. "OK, then," I said, thinking fast, "then we just have to deal with the spot, right?"

"I guess," she said with hope in her bloodshot eyes. Could I actually save her?

Esperanto. I could. I knew exactly what to do. "We just need something to put around your waist, you know, like when it's too hot and you tie a jumper or something around your waist, with the arms?" I looked at her.

"I don't have a jumper," she said. "Do you?"

"No," I said, "but wait a minute." I took a breath, thinking. I didn't trust anyone in the whole school, except maybe Pam. But I was determined to find her help.

I stepped back into the hall at just the right moment. Coming out of the office was a boy wearing jeans, a black T-shirt, and a long-sleeved shirt. Perfect! I waved at him.

When he came closer, I said, "Uh, Sam?" This just might work, I thought. Sam was so different. He brought in colourful leaves and pressed them dry on the radiator. When we'd done the Angel Network, he was the one who made the glitter card. He was an expert in plaiting, and even the snottiest cheerleader-type wanted him to do her hair at breaktime.

Sam raised a hand. "*Saluton?*" he said. My language! He'd been paying attention!

I smiled, reached out, and... pulled him right into the girls' bathroom.

"Um... wait! What? You guys need something?" he asked. Startled, he hung back. Pam, paler than ever, froze. Sam looked at her and, moving with care, took a long step back towards the door.

I waved at Pam, who was trying to shrink into the wall. She looked like she might faint. "She needs like a shirt or jumper or something before she can come out."

Here's the tremendous thing about Sam: he didn't ask why. He immediately stripped off the denim shirt he was wearing over his T-shirt and handed it over.

I tied it around Pam's waist, arranging it to cover the blot. She was doubtful. "It looks fine," I said. "No one will notice." I glanced at Sam who was already half out the door.

"You look OK," he said to Pam quickly. "Really." And then he was gone. Pam and I stared at one another, and then we both burst out laughing. He'd been so eager to escape! Something clicked for me right then, like a dial finally turned to the right position.

"*Esperanto*," I said to Pam. I told her about my mantra. She listened, nodded. We looked into each other's eyes and said it together.

Pam walked out with me right behind her. It was between classes, and we just melted back in with no questions asked. No one noticed anything.

The next day, when it was lunchtime, I found Pam. Before we reached the art studio, I tapped her arm and pointed at her lilac lunch box. "Want to try the cafeteria?" I asked. She shrugged, but came with me.

The low roar of voices inside the lunchroom was a physical wall that we had to push through. I paused and searched for two empty seats. Then, I saw someone with space on either side. It was Sam.

He'd spread his lunch out: a pear, cubes of cheese, half a baguette. He looked up, saw me... and waved! I looked behind me. No one there. At us! He had waved at us.

I hesitated. Sitting with a boy was not something I thought I'd be doing. Not in public. Not here. Beside me Pam said in a quiet voice, "*Esperanto*."

"Let's do it," I said. She didn't hesitate. We both sat down.

"*Saluton!*" Sam said, raising his carton of apple juice. "So, Carmela, what's with this language thing, anyway?"

I started to answer, "I can teach you some words, if you like. It's..." I stopped myself. I remembered how Elizabeth had turned away from me before. With care, I checked Sam's face, then Pam's. Sam, his eyes serious, looked interested. Pam just smiled and dug into a tangerine.

When I didn't go on, she looked up. "It sounds neat."

I grinned and said, "But first, I'm starving."

Now that we had our own space, there would be time to talk later. About Esperanto. About everything. After lunch.

Dear Meena

Angela Kanter

Monday

Dear Meena,

Since you have left me to go on this stinking school trip on my own, I am having to share a dorm with:

1. Cathy – spends all her free time on the bed eating those bright orange cheese puffs that smell like feet and analysing herself with magazine quizzes.

2. Rachel – has huge feet that smell like bright orange cheese puffs. Rachel SINGS all the time in this dead gruff voice, with her headphones on, so she can't hear herself when she goes out of tune. All the clothes she has brought with her are a disgusting sludge green or luminous yellow and made of waterproof stuff – I bet she even has pyjamas to match.

3. Namita – she is teeny, with long, dark, shiny

hair, and she has a whole line-up of disinfectant sprays and wipes by her bed, in case she has to step in any cow poo on country walks, etc. She keeps nagging us to tidy up or we won't win the dorm prize (as if we wanted to). She does teeny-tiny cross-stitch sewing, like a Victorian child.

Of course, you know WHY I am sharing with these leftover, dreggy people who I don't specially want to get to know. Because you aren't here – and your name was the only one I put on my List of People You Want To Share With. After all, you are supposed to be my best friend. And I am Very, Very Angry that you haven't come.

I deserve to have you here. Didn't I let you do surgery on my Secret Princess Fashion Doll when we were four? And when we were ten, I made up all those great excuses for you whenever you didn't hand in your homework on time. Well, Ms Lowry believed most of them. It was only really that one about the green hand reaching out through the drain and snatching your schoolbag that she didn't go for. And that one about accidentally eating your worksheet in your sleep.

I wish I was in Nightingale Dorm with Lydia Porchetti. She looks like a Secret Princess Fashion

Doll herself. She has three pairs of these really cool boots – one lilac, one sand-coloured and one dark chocolate. And a fur-lined anorak, so she doesn't get cold on the foul field walks. And a fur hat to match.

Rachel says she heard that Lydia's dorm have all brought their mobiles and put them under this loose floorboard, so they can text each other after lights-out. And Lydia's promised to have all the people in her dorm to her mega-sleepover when we get back home. Her brother will be there – the one who's in Crush. You know – the one with the floppy hair who makes you go all funny when you see him on TV. Lydia is worth knowing. Not like Cathy, Rachel and Namita.

I've only been here six hours and I've sprained my wrist already. I hope you feel sorry for me. It happened when I was being extremely daring on the obstacle course. Lydia Porchetti was well impressed and is probably trying to get me transferred to her dorm right this minute so she can personally nurse me.

Actually, that's not true. It happened when I got out of the coach and tripped over Lydia's four pieces of matching pastel leather luggage. It was the small make-up case. Lydia's gang had a good laugh at me. That's OK – they are simply learning to appreciate that I am an amusing person to have around.

Have to stop writing now, as we are going to do an assault course. Miss Pig-Face Piggott told me I could still join in with all the humiliating team games and that it would be a Lesson In Cooperation for them to help their Less Able Team Member. Namita straightaway volunteered to help me the whole time, which wasn't very kind of her, because I was hoping Lydia Porchetti would be filled with pity for me and decide to be my partner.

I couldn't believe it when Mum said that all new girls would have to go on an Outdoor Insanity Week. Sorry – I mean Outdoor Activity Week. But I thought I could bear it, because you would be with me. Hmph! Why do schools think that this sort of torture is a good way to meet people? I would meet them much better if they shut us in a room full of cushions, with unlimited chocolate milkshakes and double-chocolate fudge cake. I hope you are pleased with yourself, lying around like a princess while I prance around with this bunch of loonies.

Your Abandoned Friend,

Emma

PS Things I Would Like Returned:

My bubblegum lip tint
My Crush CD
The sparkly scrunchie I lent you in Year 4 for the disco

Tuesday
Dear Meena,

Today we are going rafting. I wish you were here. If I drown, I will never know what it's like to fit into my silver top properly without having to stuff it with tissues (sob!). And who's going to look after my cuddly toy collection? If you were here, you could have them. Maybe I should leave them to Lydia Porchetti, although she has no need of them. Then she will realise that she should have chosen me for a friend.

Perhaps Lydia will fall off her raft and I will save her from drowning and she will invite me to be her best friend and join her dorm.

We're back from rafting. Rachel had been rafting ten times before and she was really bossy about it. Luckily I couldn't row or anything, with my rotten wrist. Pig-Face looked at me as if I'd busted my wrist deliberately to skive off. When actually it is YOU who are skiving off.

I noticed that Lydia was nodding away and

sniggering to her lot in the background. Namita says they were laughing at Rachel's anorak. Well – that's fair enough. She looked like a cross between Father Christmas and a sack of potatoes.

Lydia's fur hat fell in the water, so I tried to lean over and get it. Fell overboard by accident. Rachel pulled me out, Namita helped me to dry my clothes and Cathy sustained me with a bag of glow-in-the-dark cheese puffs.

Lydia Porchetti's team came first in the rafting race. She wouldn't take her hat back, either. She said it was an old one she'd worn specially in case it got ruined. She threw it at me and it hit me right in the chest and made a big brown splodge on Namita's pink top which she'd just lent me.

I suppose you've spent all day lounging in front of the TV.

More humiliation tonight. A quiz with forfeits. Rachel is singing again. I will probably have to be on their team. Without you and your encyclopaedic knowledge of chart hits and nail-varnish shades, we will never be able to win. IT IS SO TOTALLY UNFAIR.

Your Abandoned Friend,

Emma

PS Rachel lent me her pineapple soap to take the stink of the river away. Namita said she would lend me her anti-bacterial shower gel, but I didn't want to smell like a hospital. No offence.

Remember when I gave you that strawberry bubble bath for your birthday and I'd just tried a teeny bit first to see how it smelt and then stuck sticky tape round the lid? And you turned the parcel upside down and it leaked all over a book someone else gave you?

Why aren't you here, stupid?

Your A.F.

E

Wednesday

Dear Meena,

Amazingly, we won the quiz. Namita knew all the answers, even though the questions were extraordinarily difficult ones like, "What is the capital of Slovenia?"(I can't spell the answer, but it's something like "Lovely-Bubbles".)

I simply have to be invited to Lydia Porchetti's sleepover! Thought maybe I don't look cool enough, so I decided to take very great care with my outfit for today's long hike to Castle Hill. Best birthday boots (knee-high black suede), skirt to match – and that big black chenille sweater that makes me look like a rock star.

I spent another hour doing my hair and missed

breakfast.

As soon as we all assembled outside the huts after breakfast, the instructors handed out these big baggy red and yellow waterproofs with hoods, so that we looked like a load of Teletubbies. I decided to walk alongside Lydia and impress her with my intellectual conversation instead. But I couldn't work out which one she was – we all looked the same in our Teletubby suits. I picked someone at random and I'd been talking to them about modern art for twenty minutes before she offered me a cheese puff and I realised it was Cathy.

After about another twenty minutes, the heel came off one of my boots and water started seeping into the other one.

After another twenty, I started to feel really weak and dizzy and I sat down on a tree root. Namita hung around staring at me, but when I tried to tell her to go away, I went all woozy and fainted. Must've been because I was too busy doing my hair to have breakfast.

Next thing I knew, I was lying on my back in the mud being shouted at by Pig-Face and laughed at by Lydia Porchetti.

"You are spoiling this walk for everybody else!" was Pig-Face's caring remark as she hauled me to my feet.

Cathy gave me some more cheese puffs and Rachel gave me some dry socks from her rucksack and Namita put her arm under mine and sort of dragged me the rest of the way.

It rained all afternoon and the castle was so old it had no roof on, so there was no place to shelter. On the way back, Lydia Porchetti actually spoke to me. She said, "You have cheese puffs stuck to your teeth."

Don't suppose you have time to think about me. My wrist aches. So does my heart.

Your Abandoned Friend,

Emma

PS More Things You Need To Give Back To Me:

The friendship bracelet I made you out of torn-up rough book in geog. when we were bored.

All the cash you have ever borrowed for emergency sweets, chocolate, mags etc.

The exercise book where we drew the flat we were going to share together when we were twenty. I shall be sharing with Lydia Porchetti by then, I expect. She is bound to notice me soon. When I win the talent competition. Haven't a clue what I am going to do, but I am sure I will think of something.

Thursday

Dear Meena,

Namita hung around waiting for me to make sure I didn't miss breakfast, so I had to sit next to her, even though there was a seat free next to Lydia Porchetti. Cathy sat opposite and ate a bowl of cornflakes big enough for an elephant. Does she only eat orange stuff? Perhaps that's how she keeps her hair that colour. Her jumper was orange, too.

I have decided to do that Indian dance you taught me last Diwali for the talent show. It won't be as good without you, but since you didn't come, I suppose there's nothing I can do about it, is there?

Rachel and Namita and Cathy are going to do this totally humiliating song in harmony, which they made up, all about the activity week and how it helps us overcome our problems and be friends together. It's called "Obstacle Course".

They asked me if I wanted to be in it, but I said no, thanks, I was going to do a dance that someone taught me who Used To Go Everywhere With Me But Is Not Actually Here When I Need Them Most.

"Oh, so that's what's the matter with you," said Namita. "We wondered."

"*We wondered! We wondered!* Have you been

talking about me behind my back?" I demanded.

"Yes, we have," said Namita. "Do you want to talk about it?"

"*NOOOOOOOO!*" I screamed and I ran out of the room and smack into Lydia Porchetti. She got a black eye, so she's going to look like a panda in the talent competition. I was ever so caring and offered to get ice for it, but her friends from Nightingale all pushed me out of the way.

Pig-Face came to do first aid and when she saw me, she said, "Not you again, Emma. Dear, dear. I have been most concerned by your attitude on this trip. I know that you have been unhappy without your best friend from primary school, but you really must behave more maturely."

Namita stuck up for me and explained it was an accident.

"Just go and get ready for rock climbing," said Pig-Face.

So, from Pig-Face to the rock face.

I don't like heights very much, but rock climbing was yet another thing that Rachel and Cathy seemed to love and they were very quick at it. Namita and I got a bit left behind. Then Namita said she felt sick and it wasn't that she'd had too many of Cathy's cheese puffs. She said she was scared of heights and I had to yell for Pig-Face to come and she brought Bob the instructor – and they hauled Namita up onto a grassy ledge and told me to sit with her.

We sat and watched the others finishing the climb. I was particularly staring at Lydia and feeling hopeless. I didn't have a chance of getting invited to her sleepover.

Namita saw I was staring at Lydia.

"Wouldn't waste your time on her," she said. "She was at my last school – if she doesn't want to know you, she can be... You know."

I explained that Lydia's brother's in Crush and I wanted to get invited to her sleepover, so I could meet him, but Namita just made a face.

Then Namita started asking about you – who were you? Why was I writing to you? Were you coming to the High School? Why weren't you on the trip? Did we have a row? Stuff like that.

"I don't want to talk about it," I said.

"Oh, you must," said Namita. "You have to take my mind off how high we are, or I swear I'm going to puke, Emma."

D'you know, I've only just thought of this, but I bet Namita was faking the whole thing. She wasn't scared of heights. She just wanted to make me talk about you. But I guess it was a relief to tell somebody.

I told Namita how you were – how you *are* my best friend – but then, like an idiot, I started to cry. It seemed safer to go back to talking about Lydia.

"The only reason I wanted to get friendly with Lydia was to get her brother's autograph for Meena," I said. "And maybe some tickets to Crush's next concert. Something she could look forward to."

And then I had to tell her. How I've been so scared in case you died. I kicked the cliff. I needed to move the pain from my chest to somewhere else where it wouldn't choke me so much.

Namita thought I was crazy. "Why do you think your friend might die?" she said. "It's us doing the dangerous stuff, here on the cliffs!"

I explained how you needed new lungs and a new heart. I told her how you had to be on a waiting list – and then when the hospital called you, you had to rush off to have your operation, the day before the school trip. I wanted to stay with you – but Mum said it would be better to come here and take my mind off things. But it drives me crazy that you're ill. I feel so angry all the time. And I'm scared.

"I'm scared too," said Namita. "Scared of this cliff!"

So I helped her finish the climb and we didn't have to talk about you anymore just then.

This evening, I didn't feel like doing the dance

in the talent show, so I joined in with the song and dance that Rachel, Cathy and Namita were doing. I knew all the moves and the words. They'd bored me stiff practising it in the dorm. We didn't win, but Pig-Face actually came up and said we were "jolly good".

Lydia Porchetti's dorm got caught having a midnight feast. Pig-Face is going to tell Lydia's mum and she might not be allowed to have her sleepover party. She had a big row with the other Nightingales, saying it was their fault they got caught, because they'd made too much noise. All their mobiles got confiscated, too!

I didn't mean what I said in those letters. I don't want any of my stuff back. I was just angry. It's lucky, really, that I'd forgotten to bring stamps, so I couldn't post my letters anyway. They're still in our dorm. Our awfully tidy, prize-winning dorm.

As soon as they let me see you, I'm coming over with my photos of the trip. I might bring Namita. I'm sure you'd like her and when you're well enough to come to the High School, we can all sit together – you, me, Namita, Rachel and Cathy.

Hope you like cheese puffs.

Can't wait to see you again.

Your Friend, always,

Emma

The Middle Ground

BELINDA HOLLYER

It goes right back to my first day at school when the whole class of us newbies was lined up in the playground outside Mrs Mercer's room, ready to be marched inside and start our new lives as scholars. I wouldn't have admitted it out loud, I knew it wasn't cool to enjoy school, but I was seriously excited that morning. I'd been excited for weeks. Every time something school-related was mentioned, an extra rush of fizzy expectation bubbled up inside me. And now, finally, there I was, with a brand-new pencil case in my bag and brand-new ribbons on my plaits. I couldn't wait to encounter all the things I thought I'd learn. School things. Things I didn't even know that I didn't know.

"You'll learn so much I won't recognise you when I see you again!" Dad had said the night before. "When you come home tomorrow, you'll be a different girl, Laurie. You'll know—" he hesitated for a moment, thinking, and I nudged him impatiently.

"What? What will I know?"

"You'll know – about the great Pacific

explorers," he said, quick as a flash, so I knew he was making it up. Dad always talks too fast when he's stuck for the truth. "And you'll know – how to make pompoms! And you'll be able to do really complicated sums, like 'gazinters'."

I just blinked at him. My older sister Nola had made pompoms at school and Dad knew I longed to do the same. I was willing to take his news about the great explorers on trust. But I'd never heard of gazinters.

"You know, Laurie, like 'eight gazinter sixteen twice'."

I blinked again. I still didn't get his joke, if you can call it one, and he laughed and kissed me on the nose, and called me his little gazinter. I knew he was teasing me but I didn't mind. Back then, Dad was the only person in the whole world who could tease me without me bursting into floods of tears.

"Go for it, Laurie! Knock 'em dead!" he called out as he left for work the next morning.

Anyway, like I said, there I was, about halfway down the girls' line outside the classroom. I was excited and nervous and trying to seem casual, all at the same time. I was also sneaking quick peeks around me, trying to work out which of the girls might turn out to be my best friend, because I was looking forward to having one. Nola had a best friend – in fact she was on her third best friend in two years. They went around together, they dressed the same, they even giggled in the same high-pitched tone. They had secret clubs only they were allowed to join. It was all the usual stuff, but it wasn't usual to me then, and I longed to do it too.

I was so curious to see who'd be my best friend that it never occurred to me to wonder if I'd find one, or worry that I wouldn't. Self-doubt didn't feature in my mind when I was six, which now I think about it probably means I wasn't all that well prepared for school.

I was keeping my eye on a girl with curly red hair who was standing at the front of the line. She reminded me of the heroine in a story my mother was reading to me, so I thought she'd probably make excellent best-friend material. I was imagining the two of us cosied up together by lunchtime when there was a tug – a sharp and painful tug – on one of my plaits. It came from behind me. If you've ever had plaits, you'll know how much it hurts when a strand of hair gets caught in something. Well, it was like that.

It wasn't only a lack of self-doubt that I brought to school that day. I also wasn't used to anyone hurting me on purpose. Nola slapped me sometimes if I took her things without asking, but it wasn't ever a hard slap, and we got along fine as a general rule. Mum had once clipped me on the leg when I'd been rude to her, but almost immediately she'd burst into tears, asked me to forgive her, and said she'd never lift a finger to me again. And Dad? He never hurt anyone or anything that I ever knew about. So more than anything, I was surprised by the tug.

When I turned around, there stood Wilma Martin. I didn't know her name then. I just saw a tall girl with freckles and little slitty eyes, holding up one of the ribbons from my plaits and waving it in my face. She'd ripped it right off, rubber band and all! No wonder it hurt.

This was my first encounter with Wilma, and I knew nothing about her, no matter how suggestive her mean expression might have been. So I just stared back at her, holding on to my other plait to keep it out of her grasp. I might not have known much about hurting people on purpose, but one look at Wilma told me that she was trouble. (The next year, when we were playing basketball, Wilma threw the ball so hard at me that it broke my arm. By then I knew she'd done it on purpose; she's just a nasty person. But back then, I didn't know.)

Wilma glanced over her shoulder to make sure

that Mrs Mercer wasn't on her way across the playground. Then she stuck her tongue out at me and grabbed for my other plait. When she couldn't reach it because I was holding it so tightly, she pulled back her fist to punch me. It was clear, even to me, that she meant business.

So I knocked her over.

I honestly didn't mean to. Afterwards I wondered if I'd taken Dad's advice to knock 'em dead too seriously, but I think it was just a chance shot. Beginner's luck. Whatever. What I'm saying is, I lashed out in her direction to get her away from me and I caught her by surprise — mine as well as hers.

My fist didn't hurt Wilma but it got her off balance. She pulled away from it, stumbled, and went down on the asphalt. Not everyone would have noticed, except that Wilma made a sort of *ouuf*! sound when she hit the ground and the whole class turned around and gawped. No one said anything for several moments. It was like a dream, or a film with the soundtrack on mute. I just stood there wondering what would happen next.

Wilma didn't stay down for long, of course. She scrambled back up and advanced towards me with evil intent written all over her face. The other kids were making bets or taking sides by now, and some of the boys even started to form a circle around the two of us, like we were prize fighters. Frankly, I felt sick, and the only reason I didn't turn and run was that I was more or less glued to the spot in panic.

But then two things happened.

Wilma was so busy giving me her full-on evil hex look that she didn't look where she was going.

And Ken Goldsworthy, whom I'd also never met before but who happened to be across from me in the boys' line, stepped forward and tripped her up.

Just like that. On purpose. To stop her from hitting me back.

After Wilma landed on the asphalt for the second time Ken grinned at me. Then he turned back to her, grabbed the ribbon she was still clutching, and handed it back to me. It was – oh, it was *really* like a full-on film then. Thinking back now, I can just about hear the swoopy background music.

When Mrs Mercer finally bustled across the playground to usher us into her classroom, the lines of boys and girls had reformed and everyone was waiting quietly. Although Wilma had a graze on her elbow she didn't say anything about how it had happened. She was so surprised at being knocked down twice without getting in even one swing herself, she didn't fully recover her meanness for several days.

And me? I'd fallen in love.

Love him? Of course I loved him. I don't mean soppy hearts and flowers or any Valentine's Day nonsense, I mean I loved him like a friend. A-boy-who-was-a-friend, not a *boyfriend*. Ken had more or less saved my life, and if that didn't make him my best friend I didn't know what would.

I'd never thought my best friend would turn out to be a boy. In my imaginings it was always a girl, making pompoms together and working out the secret rules for our exclusive club. But for Ken, I put my plans for me and Bonnie (Ms Curly Red Hair) into the second division.

If boyfriends *had* been in my universe at that stage, Ken might have made a good one. He had a honey-brown tan and blond hair that fell into his brown eyes. He was tall and lanky, like a farm boy in a movie: handsome, but not drop-dead gorgeous. At six, of course, I didn't rate boys for their attractiveness. Now I can see that Ken was – well, not exactly dashing, but not a waste of space either. But all I knew then was, he was my best friend.

I have to wonder what he thought he was doing

when he saved me from Wilma. Was it compassion for the underdog? Or because he didn't like bullies? Did he actually *want* me for a friend, with the same absolute certainty I wanted him for one? I never asked myself any of that at the time and I never asked Ken either, I just sort of claimed him.

I stuck to him all the rest of that first day. I handed him a bottle of milk at break, I sat beside him to eat my lunch, I took the easel next to his for painting, and I was cross-legged beside him on the mat at story-time. He didn't look surprised about any of that and he didn't edge away or complain. In fact, after the first few times he saved a space for me.

Maybe he felt he'd won me in a fair fight? Like a knight in a story who wins the hand of a fair princess? Except that Ken didn't know that sort of story; he was more into video games. Maybe he simply went along with it all to keep me happy. He was always very kind-hearted.

My mother didn't know what to make of my news that afternoon. She'd probably expected me to be a girly girl like my sister, so when I rushed in to tell her that my best friend's name was Ken, she looked surprised. But then again, she'd had six years of me wanting to wear shorts instead of skirts, and wanting to be with Dad when he made things in the shed instead of with her when she cooked or sewed. So no surprise really – I wasn't even slightly into pink back then. Dad just grinned, and said something about the pompoms being on hold.

At school Ken and I played together, but not all the time. On occasions, I played hopscotch with Bonnie, and Ken played do-or-die soldier stuff with the other boys. Bonnie was fun, and when the girls had to pair off for anything I always tried to get her as my partner. But mostly Ken and I did everything together. I was the only girl in Ken's gang, which the other boys never questioned. He was the only guest at my birthday party when I turned seven, because he was the only person I wanted to invite. Everyone accepted that we were besties; that if you saw one of us the other one'd be along in a minute.

We rode our bikes down to the beach at the weekends and practised overarm and backstroke in the sea until our fingers went all crinkly. We went fishing with Ken's dad, who called me Missy but was otherwise OK. During the week we'd go to my place after school so Ken could teach our new spaniel puppy to do tricks. Amber was never big on unnecessary effort, not even back then, but she finally rocked back and flipped a front paw up into a high five when he asked her to. We shot hoops in his backyard because that's where the hoop was, and we did wheelies on our bikes in his road because there was never any traffic there. We did our homework together too, side by side: maths at my place because Dad was good at helping, once he got past the gazinter jokes, and composition at Ken's because his mum was magic at inventing stories.

Maybe there's a middle ground between, say, hopscotch and space invaders? Well, Ken and I lived in that space.

But when I was ten, almost eleven, it started to change.

I started to notice things about myself, things that had been going on for a while but I hadn't paid them much attention. Like, I wanted to spend more time with Bonnie. Not just a partner for cookery class or the girls-only Maori poi dance; other stuff too. I discovered that hanging out with her after school was good fun. We'd go down to the shops together and look at outrageous outfits that our mothers would hate. We'd sit and have milkshakes and talk about pop stars and what was on TV. We'd go to the library and borrow the next two books in a series we were reading, and then swap with each other during the week.

I didn't want to do any of that with Ken.

I felt awkward and disloyal and I knew I'd started, ever so slowly, to drift away from him.

The crunch finally came when Bonnie's ex-best-friend, Maureen, teamed up with Wilma. Wilma had never forgotten our first schoolday and she blamed me for her humiliation, even though the whole thing had clearly been her fault. Even breaking my arm in basketball hadn't satisfied her desire for revenge.

So Maureen and Wilma ganged up on me and Bonnie. Nothing very bad, but they'd talk about us like we were babies who didn't know anything important, right in our faces like we weren't there. Then they'd go on about having boyfriends and kissing, and it made me feel sort of weird. As though I'd been dropped on a strange new planet and didn't understand the language.

One day Bonnie and I were sitting watching the boys play touch football, and Wilma and Maureen flounced up and started going on – about boys, of course. And when Ken saw me and waved, I waved back. That was all they needed, and they pounced like predators.

"You *like* him!" Giggle giggle, nudge nudge.

Well, yeah! But what I meant wasn't what they meant, and we all knew it.

I wanted to belong. I was nervous and unsure of myself but I sort of wanted to try out their world – see what it felt like, how it tasted; something like that.

So I said, "No, I don't! I don't like him at all."

And the word spread like a bush fire in summer. *Laurie doesn't like Ken anymore!*

It tipped the whole thing over on its head and I didn't know how to get it straight. I lost my whole sense of direction, like an explorer adrift on the ocean without a map.

The next day Ken caught my arm as we were going into class. He looked strained and embarrassed, and his smile was tense around the edges, like when he thought he'd be called on in class.

"Laurie," he said quietly. "I have to know if you still like me."

I didn't say anything at first. I just looked at him.

And everyone looked at me. It couldn't have been everyone, actually. It probably wasn't more than one or two people. But I was out in the arena, and I didn't like it.

What's more, I could feel Wilma and Maureen standing behind me, eyes on stalks, holding their breath.

So I laughed. It came out as a tinkling laugh, like girls sometimes do together. The memory sends chills down my spine.

"No, Ken," I said. "No, I don't." And I giggled again. This time it sounded like breaking glass.

It was a betrayal. I knew it as soon as I said it. I knew it when I looked at Ken's face and saw confusion there. Pain and confusion.

Why didn't I put it right then and there?

All I know is that I didn't. I told myself I'd explain the next time Ken and I were together, but that didn't happen. He didn't wait for me after school anymore, and he didn't come round on his bike. I rode past his house from time to time as slowly as I dared, but his bike was never there and I never got up enough courage to knock.

Dad said it was just a girl thing and not to worry. Mum hugged me when I cried about it and said that growing up could be painful. Only I knew how badly I'd behaved. It was only a little thing I'd said, just a few words. But I'd hurt him on purpose, and been so mean-spirited I still blush just thinking about it.

At the end of that year we were split up by the education system – Ken went to Westlake Middle School and I went to Peary Fowler. Sometimes I saw him in the distance at basketball games and waved, but I don't know if he saw me. He never waved back.

And after that – well, to be honest, I forgot about him after that. Through high school, and starting uni, and then going flatting in town with Bonnie. So it wasn't until last Saturday that I remembered it all.

Nola and I were home for the weekend because Amber died. We were trying to cheer Mum and Dad up, maybe even talk them into getting a new puppy to take their minds off it. And Dad and I were looking through old photos of Amber – and suddenly there she was, a puppy herself, doing her high five with Ken. Both of them were laughing at the camera.

I sat for a minute or two, staring at the photo while Dad went on talking. Then I picked it up, and borrowed Nola's car, and went round to Ken's place to give it to him. But the whole family had moved to the South Island – years ago, according to the new people in his house. They didn't have a forwarding address anymore.

Ken Goldsworthy, if you're out there and if you ever read this – I want to tell you I'm sorry.

The Swing Chair

NORMAN SILVER

At Pumla's house, next door to ours, there's a three-seater swing chair on the veranda, overlooking the street. It has seats and a canopy covered with a faded floral material, which I'm sure was fashionable in the Stone Age. It was on that swing chair that Pumla and I spent many hours, chatting about boys, clothes, hair, teachers – but mostly about boys. Because we were such good friends, we knew each other's taste in boys. And we shared all our experiences. I knew all the secrets of her love life, and she knew all the secrets of mine – which, to tell the truth, were not that many, as I hadn't yet found a boy I really clicked with.

That swing chair was old. I know for a fact Pumla's parents hadn't bought it, because it was on that veranda when the previous owners lived there. The two of them used to love sitting on that chair. Then one day they won over a million rand in the Lotto, and immediately they became Mr and Mrs Posh, and relocated to a smarter area.

When the Matsabas moved in, I was overjoyed to see a girl my age in the family. That was Pumla, and we became good friends immediately. From the start, I liked her mother and father, who welcomed me into their house as if I was part of their family. It was from that time onwards that Pumla and I used to sit most afternoons on the swing chair, watching the world and its dogs go past on the pavement.

We used to sway gently, with our feet resting on the floor tiles, propelling us lazily back and forth in time to the creaking of the rusty hinges. Pumla's veranda was higher than ours, and from there you could see from the Portuguese shop at the bottom corner all the way up to where Michael lived in the house at the top of the hill.

Both Pumla and I were madly infatuated with Michael. Michael the beautiful. Michael the brave. Michael the beloved. Everyone in the street knew the story of Michael. He and his father, with no money, had walked all the way from Nigeria. His father was bitten by a snake, they were attacked by thugs in Kinshasa, they endured torturous days without food or water, but somehow they survived and made it to Johannesburg, City of Gold.

When they arrived, they were taunted by the locals, who swore at them for coming here to steal their work. But slowly, Michael's father set up a business selling Nigerian masks, and now he had a prestigious stall at the Rosebank Rooftop Market and was married to a woman from Zimbabwe.

Speak to any girl in Bez Valley and their eyes would flutter at the mention of Michael. He was tall and well-built, his skin was shiny and the expression on his face was that of someone who had gone through a lot and come out victorious. His deep black eyes sparkled when he spoke and you just wished that you could know him better.

As far as Pumla and I were aware, a stream of girls had passed through Michael's life, each of them hoping to get more than just acquainted. But he hadn't hooked up with any in a serious long-term relationship.

"How can we get Michael to notice us?" Pumla and I would muse desperately, as we sat on the swing chair.

We were both two years younger than him, and at a different school. How could we ever worm our way into the life of a demigod like Michael?

Opposite Pumla's house was the Sunset Home for the Elderly. From our swing chair, we couldn't help but notice their daily routines. It was run by Belinda, with platinum hair, gold high heels and short leopard-print mini-skirts. She looked glamorous, but when you got close up, you could tell she was over fifty, and had been face-lifted and boob-lifted. Still, she did her job well, because in the time that we've lived on Protea Street, she bought up another house nearby, and one beyond that, and turned them also into Sunset Homes. I'm sure if you check out this street in thirty years time, it will be nothing but Sunset Homes. Maybe the next street also. The place could be swarming with people in zimmer frames and wheelchairs, with Belinda at eighty-five, still in her leopard-print mini-skirt, looking more glamorous than ever.

Pumla and I knew a few of the elderly residents by sight and we would always greet them when they passed by. One day, an old fellow who was being pushed along in a wheelchair by his nurse, surprised me by asking me to marry him. His hunched-over wife stood beside him.

I thought he was just joking, so I said, "OK, if my dad and ma agree."

"Well, you go ask them," he said.

I laughed, and went inside.

The next time the old man saw me, he said, "Oh, here's the girl I'm going to marry."

I giggled, but suddenly the old man's wife piped up, speaking with a shrill voice. "You can marry who you want, you stupid man. I've had enough of you anyway. I can get any man I want."

I made a quick exit, leaving them arguing on the pavement. Pumla laughed when I told her what happened.

"Well, at least you've had a proposal of marriage," she joked. "Nobody has ever proposed to me."

We sat there rocking on the swing chair in the late afternoon sun.

"I'll never be able to love anyone other than Michael," she said suddenly. "He's so gorgeous."

She closed her eyes dreamily, no doubt imagining herself in Michael's arms. I didn't blame her. I had done that myself often enough. But I thought her words were a little melodramatic.

"I think of him all the time," she said. "I'm just waiting for the right moment to get his attention."

I must admit I felt a touch jealous as she spoke. Pumla was much more attractive and more sociable than me. I was sure that she would be noticed by Michael long before me. But despite this, I still had a small hope tucked away that I could one day be Michael's girlfriend – even if it meant that Pumla would lose out.

But how could these idle hopes ever become reality? Never in our wildest dreams would we have imagined that Doctor Silk would intervene on our behalf.

Just past the Sunset Homes was a house in ruins. The gutters were falling off, the paintwork was peeling, the garden was wild. This was Doctor Silk's residence. I had hardly ever seen him. I don't think anyone on the street really knew him. When we were young, we were frightened to go near his house because we believed he was mad and ate children. As we grew older we heard rumours that he was perverted, and had murdered a woman.

One evening, Pumla and I were chatting on the swing chair, when suddenly we saw Doctor Silk come running out of his house in shorts and a vest. He made a beeline for the Sunset Homes, but then spotted the two of us sitting there.

"Hey, you girls!" he called out. "Where's Phineas?"

Phineas was the security guard for the Sunset Homes, minding the property and making sure that none of the old biddies escaped. Usually he sat on the opposite pavement, listening to jazz and township music on a tinny radio.

"He's probably taken a wheelchair to one of the old people," I replied.

"Listen… sorry to disturb you… maybe you girls can help me… I can't work while that monster's in there."

"What monster?" Pumla asked.

"Parktown prawn. Big one!" he answered, holding out his fingers to show a creature about the size of his fist. "Biggest one I've ever seen. I can't touch those things. Please... can you help me get rid of it?"

Parktown prawns, I can tell you now, are not delicious, edible prawns. They're not even prawns at all. They're huge orange insects.

"I'll chuck it out for you," I answered.

Pumla was not keen on Parktown prawns either, but she accompanied Doctor Silk and me back to his house. He wouldn't go in the front door.

"It's in the study. Big fat one."

Pumla also seemed nervous. I don't know if she was more frightened of the Parktown prawn or Doctor Silk's evil reputation. She whispered that she would keep guard at the front door so that he didn't lock me in.

I stepped inside cautiously. You had to be cautious, to avoid the piles of papers and books that lined both sides of the passage. When I looked into the lounge, similar piles covered the whole carpet. I made my way to the study like an intrepid hunter. There it was in the corner – a truly huge Parkie, with spiky legs and powerful mandibles.

I tipped out some pens from a glass jar that stood on the desk and, with a ball-point, timidly coaxed the Parkie away from the wall. As I did so, I heard someone coming into the room. My heart thudded inside me – it must surely be Doctor Silk coming to do me harm.

"Hi, can I help you?"

I looked to my side and couldn't believe my eyes. It was Michael.

"Give me the jar," he said, "and you prod him towards it."

He knelt down beside me. I felt his arm brush against mine and smelled his delicious fragrance, as I goaded the Parkie. When Michael plonked the jar over it, it made a soft hiss and did a small poo.

"Phew! What a pong!" he said, grimacing, then laughing.

I found a piece of paper and slid it under the jar to act as a lid. Then Michael and I stood up.

"Good teamwork!" he said.

When Pumla saw me and Michael emerging from the house, she looked on nervously. Suddenly, Michael jolted the jar containing the Parkie towards her. She squealed in horror and backed away. Doctor Silk took even safer precautions – he ran around the corner and hid.

Michael dropped the Parkie into the drain at the side of the road.

"How come you're not frightened of creepy-crawlies?" he asked me.

"I'm just not. A Parkie doesn't bite. It is only a type of king cricket."

"You seem to know a lot about it."

"Biology is my favourite subject," I replied.

"Mine too," he said, looking intensely at me.

When they saw that the Parkie had been disposed of, Pumla and Doctor Silk bravely approached us. Doctor Silk thanked us over and over, as if we had saved him from certain death. Then he went back indoors.

"He's a great bloke," Michael said to us. "You know he used to be a top research scientist. He's made important discoveries in quantum physics."

"Whatever that is," Pumla said.

"He's still working," Michael added. "I think he often forgets to eat or sleep. I see his light on sometimes, right through the night. Listen, would you girls like to come up to the square for a burger or something?"

While we walked up to the café, we chatted and laughed together. During our snack, Michael told us he was working hard for his matric, because he needed first-class results to study medicine at Wits University.

"Then, after you've finished the exams, it will be time for your matric dance," Pumla said. "Are you going with your girlfriend?"

"Which girlfriend?"

"Haven't you got a girlfriend?" Pumla asked, fluttering her eyelids.

"I haven't thought about the matric dance yet," Michael said. "First things first."

By the time Pumla and I got back to the swing chair, our hearts were pounding, each with our own thoughts. Michael was just so adorable – and I liked intelligent boys.

"Jeez, did you see the way he was ogling me in the café?" Pumla remarked. "He really fancies me."

Personally, I thought it was exactly the other way round – she had done most of the ogling.

"I've got a strong feeling," she told me, "that he's going to invite me to the matric dance."

But things didn't turn out quite like she expected. Just a few days later, I got a real shock when I saw an ambulance pull up outside her house.

Oh no! I thought. *I wonder who's hurt or sick. I hope it isn't Pumla.*

I watched from our lounge window as the ambulance men carried someone from the house on a stretcher. Pumla, in a state of concern, was walking alongside. As the person on the stretcher was lifted into the ambulance, I could see it was Pumla's mother. How awful! What had happened to her? Pumla climbed up into the back of the ambulance, and then it drove off up the street.

I didn't see Pumla again till the next day, when she told me that her mom hadn't been feeling well for a few days, but then had suddenly passed out. She was still in hospital and the doctors were doing tests on her to see what was wrong. Pumla looked very tired and anxious. I held her hand and felt so much sympathy for her.

"I hope she'll get better soon," I said. "I love your mom."

Pumla spent a lot of time going back and forth to the hospital. It must have been difficult for her with her mom seriously ill, and on top of that, it was supposed to be our revision time. Pumla couldn't have been devoting much energy to her studies, while her mom was kept in hospital day after day, and then week after week.

In the meantime, Michael called me and asked if I wanted to go see a film with him on the weekend. I was naturally overjoyed and we had a great time. Afterwards we talked for ages, and it was very late before I got home. But I couldn't bring myself to tell Pumla the next morning. Why upset her when she was going through such a difficult time with her mom?

The following Friday evening, I was out with

Michael again. And we got on even better. He took me back to his house and introduced me to his dad. Then we went to his room where he showed me his shelves of science-fiction books. We sat together on his bed and listened to his favourite CDs for hours.

I couldn't bring myself to tell Pumla that Michael and I were seeing each other. Her mother's condition had not improved in all this time. Apparently the doctors had just started to administer a different medication, and Pumla hoped it would help her mother get strong enough to come home in time for Christmas.

The exams came and went. I felt certain I had done well enough to pass, but I wasn't confident about Pumla. She hadn't revised at all, and I could tell during class that her concentration was almost zero. Our teachers also noticed the change. I was seriously worried for her.

During the last week of term, Pumla caught hold of me at breaktime.

"Is it true? Tell me. Is it true?"

"Is what true?"

"You know."

"No, I don't. What?"

"Gillian said you're going to the matric dance with Michael. Is it true?"

Pumla gazed into my eyes with a ferocious, icy expression.

"Listen, Pumla, Michael and I have been getting on well…"

"So it is true. How could you do that to me? You're not a real friend," she said accusingly. "Nobody could do what you've done if they were a real friend."

I tried to explain that I hadn't wanted to hurt her while her mother was so ill.

"My mother's got nothing to do with it," Pumla moaned. "How could you do such a scaly thing to me?"

"You would have done the same," I replied.

While I spent my time trying to suss out where I could get a dress cheaply, Pumla stewed with jealousy and hurt. She refused to talk to me, and avoided my eyes if I was anywhere near her. She never sat on the swing chair anymore. It just remained there on the veranda, motionless and abandoned. There was very little I could do about it. I felt sorry for Pumla, but I also had a life to live. I couldn't jeopardise my relationship with Michael, just because of her.

The dress for the dance turned up via my cousin, who had been a bridesmaid recently. It was a fabulous lilac colour. With a little alteration, it fitted perfectly. Michael looked fantastic — smart and handsome. It was interesting to see how popular he was with all his schoolmates, and how comfortably he spoke with his teachers as he said goodbye to them. I could tell they had a very high opinion of him.

The band played some chilled tunes. The two guitar players were still at the school, and boy, were they talented! Michael and I had such a fun time and I think that night we realised there was something special between us. We had so much in common, both of us serious about making a useful contribution to our country in the future. Well, it's actually Michael's adopted country. But he said he loves it here. In Nigeria, he wouldn't have had the opportunity to go to medical school.

Just before Christmas, Pumla's mother came home. She looked so emaciated and weak, but at least the doctors felt she was able to be cared for at home. Pumla did most of the caring. She looked after her mom, cooking her healthy food and trying to cheer her up. But she deliberately avoided me. I texted her and left messages on her cell, but she just pretended I didn't exist. I just hoped that one day she and I could make up and be friends again, the way it always used to be.

Michael and I continued seeing each other. It

was still early days to say if he and I were a permanent item. But I felt a lot of love for him and I'm sure it was mutual. When we were together, it was so perfect. We both passed our exams with flying colours. Unfortunately, Pumla didn't. But because of her mother's illness, she would be allowed to sit some of them again.

After Christmas, I went round to Michael's place quite frequently, and sometimes he used to come visit me at home. On one of these occasions, we were noticed by Pumla, who was emptying some rubbish into the bin. We knew she had seen us, but she didn't wave or say hi.

Inside my room, I told Michael in detail how my friendship with Pumla had collapsed and that it broke my heart that we were no longer close.

"It's so painful. I just can't bring myself to make the first move and go speak to her."

"She's having a tough time," Michael said. "My real mother went out of my life when I was very young, so I really feel for her. But I am sure you'll get back together again. A genuine friendship won't break that easily."

In the new year, I noticed Pumla's mother up on her feet. She was walking around the house in a dressing gown. I was so pleased for her, and for Pumla. I just hoped she would continue to get well. Sometimes after that, I would see Pumla's mother sitting in their back garden with sunglasses on, reading a magazine, and my mom would greet her and make small talk over the fence about the heatwave we were having.

One day, as I was coming home from visiting Michael, I passed the old man who had wanted to marry me. When he saw me, he called out, "Should we set the date for our wedding?"

"Listen, *oupa*, you must stop saying these things, OK?" I said. "You've got a lovely wife here, who's been with you I don't know how many years. You must be nice to her."

"You see," his wife said to him in her shrill voice. "I told you she wouldn't want to marry a useless old man like you."

As I walked away from them, I heard a laugh that I hadn't heard in a long time. I looked around and there was Pumla next door, sitting on the swing chair just like old times, amused at my interaction with the old couple. I couldn't resist. I scurried along the pavement, through her front gate and onto her veranda as fast as my legs would go. I seated myself beside her and as we swayed back and forth, the rusty hinge started its familiar creaking.

Silence

Lois Metzger

Ruthie Hooper's voice always rose several octaves when she was talking to her pack of friends. "Hi! I love your blouse! What do you call that colour – lavender or lilac?" There was also the way her voice plunged several octaves to discuss something more serious. "Oh, that physics teacher and his pop quizzes! Good thing I know all about 'momentum' and 'impulse'." Ruthie, one of the popular girls. She had a large round face like a clock, and bouncy brown curls that no doubt took many hours to conjure up. Not to mention how long she must be spending on perfecting her outfits. Her jeans carefully swept the floor when she walked, and went up only so high on her hips. Her shirts came down almost, but not quite, to the top of her jeans. At school, you weren't supposed to show much skin, and Ruthie always acted as if she hadn't planned to expose several inches of her middle. "Oops!" she would say, yanking her shirt down, laughing that big loud laugh of hers.

And her oldest friend was Linda Connor. Linda – flat out beautiful. She could be a model, with those long, straight legs, the long, dark, almost-black hair that caught the light. She was brilliant, always got As. Ruthie said Linda could get As in her sleep, but Linda contradicted her; she said she had to work extra hard to keep her grades. Ruthie always laughed at this, and said, "Oh, get real!" Whenever Ruthie mentioned Linda to anyone at Gramercy High School, she always spoke of her this way: "Linda – you know, my best friend…"

Marcy Bell, a tenth-grader like Ruthie and Linda, didn't have a pack of friends. Or a best friend, either. She was so quiet, you might think she couldn't speak at all. But that wasn't it. She just chose her words, those she spoke aloud, carefully. Did her family notice? Not with three older brothers who never stopped talking. Sometimes her mother pushed Marcy's ash-blonde fringe out of her eyes and whispered gratefully, "Marcy, you're so… restful!"

Under normal circumstances, Ruthie would never waste time with Marcy. What would be the point? The girl barely said a word. Linda was always nice to Marcy, though, even though Marcy never said anything back. When Linda passed Marcy in the hall, she always said hi. If they stood next to each other in PE, playing volleyball or something, Linda was sure to say something friendly to Marcy, such as, "You made a good serve. Too bad we lost the point."

It made Marcy feel good, even though she knew Linda spoke to everybody like that.

But today was not "normal circumstances". There was going to be a school concert the following week, and at the last minute the music teacher, Mr Garnevicus, had thrown these three together to perform "Let it Be". Another trio had been rehearsing the song for a month – and now all three of them had the flu. That was just like Mr Garnevicus – not wanting an empty space in the programme. Which was conscientious of him, Marcy thought, while Ruthie considered it extra work. Ruthie played piano, Marcy played clarinet, and Linda played the flute. Marcy always thought that Ruthie, though technically correct, had no feeling for music – she just banged away at the keys.

But Linda. She played beautifully. Somehow you forgot you were watching a girl with a flute. The music seemed to float. Sometimes – Marcy never knew how she did this – Linda sounded as if she was playing *two* flutes. There was the music, and then there was something behind the music, something else. What was it? Not long ago, Marcy had heard Ruthie talking in the hall: "Linda – my best friend, you know – she's upset about her grandmother, but, I mean, come *on*. Everybody has to die. She's so old." Was Linda sad about her grandmother? Was that the something else? And Marcy never knew anyone who used silence so well. During a solo, Linda would play a series of notes and then pause, leaving you somewhere, in some other place, for several long hushed moments. Then she'd come back and take you back to where you started.

Marcy got to rehearsal first – just after 3.15, when school ended. The practice room, the Music Nook, was a kind of tiny attic at the very top of the school. Small, cramped, with a triangular ceiling like a witch's hat, an upright piano shoved next to a wall, some music stands, never enough chairs. Outside a slit of a window, which looked too small to be even called a window, gusty winds circled tall trees. Marcy took out her clarinet, put the small rectangular reed in her mouth, got it good and wet. How would they play the old Beatles song? she wondered. Soft and sweet, to highlight the flute? Or would Ruthie want to show off on the piano, slamming her feet down on the pedals, pounding the keys?

"You look like a chipmunk," Ruthie greeted her, huffing and puffing after climbing many stairs.

Marcy just looked at her.

"You don't even know, do you? You've got that thing sticking out of your mouth, like a big chipmunk tooth!"

It was true. Marcy just left the reed in her mouth sometimes, forgot it was there. She pulled it out, fastened it to the clarinet.

"Isn't Linda here yet?" Ruthie looked around.

Marcy thought that was funny. As if Linda could be hiding somewhere, in this tiny room.

"This is the *worst* day for a rehearsal. I have a zillion things to do. Let's just play it through a few times. I've got to get home."

Marcy nodded. That was fine with her. She had a mountain of homework and tests tomorrow.

Ruthie breathed out angrily, "Where the hell is Belinda?"

"*Belinda*?" Marcy said.

"That's Linda's real name. Didn't you know?"

Of course Marcy didn't know.

"She's my best friend, so I find out all kinds of privileged information stuff like that. Do you know Linda's middle name?"

Marcy shook her head.

"She doesn't have one!" Ruthie laughed her big loud laugh. "Oh, she's so late, I'm going to *kill* her when she gets here," she growled.

Marcy looked at her watch. It was only 3.22. But probably just a few minutes spent with Marcy felt like hours to Ruthie.

And then Linda came. Sometimes her beauty hit

Marcy all over again, as if she hadn't seen her only a couple of classes earlier, in PE. Her skin, for one thing. Girls put on layers of makeup to get that natural, glowing, "no makeup" look. Linda had it, without the layers. Marcy herself didn't wear makeup. A lady at a cosmetics counter had once told Marcy (who hadn't asked) that she really should because her skin was "barely there". Linda's skin — it was "all there". Linda always wore baggy jeans and button-down shirts. Nothing special. How come she always looked special?

"Sorry I'm late." Linda was not out of breath.

"Marcy here was about to leave," Ruthie said. "She was getting so angry."

"Really?" Linda looked over at Marcy, deep concern in her eyes. And Marcy saw, too, behind the concern, a sadness, settled-in, like a big puddle after a hard rain.

"No — I'm not angry," Marcy said.

"Just kidding!" Ruthie laughed. Her laugh filled the tiny room.

"Well," Linda said, "I'm sorry about this, but I can't stay and practise — "

"Why not?" Ruthie glared at her. "Hey, you don't even have your flute!"

Linda spoke softly but firmly. "That's what I'm telling you. I have to go."

"What's so important that you can't stay and rehearse for twenty minutes?" Ruthie said. "I have a lot of stuff to do, too!"

"No, you don't understand," Linda said. "I really have to go."

Marcy could see that Ruthie was extra angry because she prided herself on knowing everything about Linda. And she hadn't known about this.

"Look, Linda, you're my best friend, I love you to pieces, but you're driving me crazy. What's going on? Just tell me!"

"I have to go," Linda said, "that's all I can say. I have to go." She was clutching her music notebook, and it faced Marcy. There was a quote, or something, that Linda had scribbled on the front. *Music is better than speech. Silence is better than music.* Marcy wondered about that. It sounded like Linda wanted silence more than anything. "I'm sorry," Linda said in a voice you could hardly hear. "But I just really do – have to go."

"I know," Ruthie snapped. "You said that about a zillion times." Just as Linda turned to leave, Ruthie pulled out a necklace from under her blouse. "Hey, look, I'm wearing it."

"Oh," Linda said.

It was antique silver, covered with tiny crystals. "It's so beautiful," Marcy breathed out. She wasn't even sure she'd said this aloud.

But she must have, because Linda said, "Thank you. It belonged to my grandmother, Nina."

"And Linda gave it to *me*," Ruthie said proudly. "I love it to pieces."

"Grandma Nina just died nearly two weeks ago. That was her favourite necklace."

"But – you gave it away. Why?" Marcy asked.

Linda didn't answer straightaway.

"That's very rude!" Ruthie said. "Linda doesn't wear jewellery – haven't you noticed?"

Linda didn't react to what Ruthie had said; she just carried on talking. "It was terrible, when she died. See, I always sort of looked out for her. When she had to go somewhere, sometimes I went on a little ahead of her, to check things out, make sure everything was OK. When she died – I couldn't do that, I couldn't go on ahead anymore."

"Well, *duh*," Ruthie said.

Linda was already halfway out the door. She glanced at Ruthie, and then at Marcy. There was silence after the door closed.

And, in the silence, Marcy got it. She wasn't sure exactly how, but she did.

"Ruthie," Marcy began.

"What?"

But Marcy wasn't sure how to say it.

"*What?*" Patience was not one of Ruthie's strong points.

"Your best friend, Linda. She's... not happy."

"Oh, she's fine!"

"No, I mean, *really* not happy."

"She probably just had to handle something at home, and she didn't want to say so in front of you. Look, I know all about her family. We're related, you know. She's like my second cousin once removed, or something. Anyway, she's got this older brother. He's like thirty. My mom says the brother and the father don't speak to each other, and Linda's always in the middle. I don't know why she bothers."

"What about Linda's mother? Can't she do anything?"

"Oh, Linda's mother is completely out of it — she thinks everything is just fine. My mom says Linda's the one holding the whole family together. I think if a family wants to fall apart, let it! So, I mean, something probably came up, with the brother and the father."

"Maybe — but Linda's planning on doing something. Something really terrible."

"Like what?"

Marcy took a deep breath. "She might kill herself, Ruthie." Saying it aloud, Marcy could hear how crazy it sounded. But she knew it was true.

"That's the most – I'm not even going to dignify that with a response! I have to go to the bathroom!" This was not the exit line Ruthie would have liked, but she swept out of the tiny room. Marcy heard her stomping in the hall, the footsteps echoing. Ruthie would be back. She'd left all her stuff behind, her backpack and everything.

When she did return a few minutes later, she said, "I *hate* the bathroom on this floor. The water smells like a swimming pool. My hands are all chlorine-y."

"I know how it sounds," Marcy said.

"Well, it sounds crazy, and it is crazy. Linda's my best friend. I love her to pieces. Don't you think I'd know if she was going to kill herself?"

"She gave you her grandmother's necklace—"

"It's scratchy as hell. Don't ever tell her I said that."

"She still wants to go on ahead, to check up on her grandmother, see if she's OK."

"That's just *Linda.*"

"And she kept saying, 'I have to go.'"

"That's what people *say!*"

"Not the way she said it." Marcy frowned. "It was also… what she didn't say. The silence after the words."

"The *silence?*"

"Yes," Marcy said.

175

"Fine. I'm her best friend, we were babies together, I know everything about her, but now you know something I don't, because she used some kind of secret signal to communicate this to *you*, whom she doesn't even know!"

Well – Linda had been communicating it to both of them, only Ruthie hadn't seen or heard it. But all Marcy said, again, was, "Yes."

"You're wrong," Ruthie said, in her low-octave voice. "Dead wrong."

The room filled with silence again. Marcy could feel Ruthie's displeasure with her as if it were heat, oppressive big waves of it.

Ruthie got her stuff together.

They hadn't played one note, of course.

Ruthie opened the door, and there was the music teacher, Mr Garnevicus. He had black curly hair and a grey beard, which made him look old and young at the same time. "I was wondering how you were doing with 'Let it Be'," he said. "You're finished already? Where's Linda?"

Marcy cleared her throat.

"Linda had to go home," Ruthie said, glaring at Marcy. "'Let it Be' sounds just fine. *Let it be*, right, Marcy? Get it?"

I get it, Marcy wanted to say. *That's the whole point.*

Marcy Bell, the girl her mother called restful, did

the least restful, most talkative thing she could think of. "Mr Garnevicus," she began.

"Don't," Ruthie said.

"Don't what?" Mr Garnevicus said.

Ruthie took a step back to give herself some room. "Marcy's being a drama queen! She's got some crazy idea in her head!"

Marcy did her best to look not crazy. "I'm worried about Linda. She said some things that made me think—"

"This is ridiculous!" Ruthie broke in. "Marcy, I think you're *on* something!"

"Let her talk," Mr Garnevicus said.

And Marcy did. "Linda may try to kill herself." There. It was said. Would Mr Garnevicus think she was crazy – or on something?

"What makes you say that?" he asked matter-of-factly, after a moment.

"She kept saying she had to go, and her grandmother just died, and she gave away her grandmother's necklace—"

"To *me*," Ruthie broke in.

"—and she was sorry she couldn't see her grandmother anymore, and she couldn't make sure her grandmother was all right, and she just seemed so sad, and so lost—" Marcy took a breath. "I knew it, somehow. I felt it."

"You see?" Ruthie said. "She doesn't know what she's talking about! Linda's my best friend! If anyone knows anything about Linda Connor, it's me!"

But something in Marcy's voice, not necessarily the words, had gotten through to Mr Garnevicus. "Sounds like it might be serious," he said, turning to leave. "I'm going down to the office, talk to the school counsellor, try to take care of this right away."

"Right away? You mean *now*?" Ruthie said.

"Of course now," he said. "If it's nothing, then it's nothing. If it's something – well, that's something." He closed the door behind him.

It was just Ruthie and Marcy again, in the tiny, triangular room with its impossibly small window. And Ruthie was furious. "Linda would never, ever… You're getting her into so much trouble! Her family will be so totally freaked out! They'll probably stick her in a loony bin somewhere! And it'll be all your fault!"

Marcy just looked at her. There was nothing to say.

Sometimes it's your best friend who understands.

Sometimes it's somebody else.

Taking Flight

TESSA DUDER

She had fallen asleep even before the plane bound for Los Angeles had left the runway.

"Make the most of your window seat," her father had urged at the passengers' departure gate where they were wrenched apart. "You might see the coastline as you gain height and head off towards Greenland. Wave to Granny in her garden. She sees the planes go over, remember… Got your ticket, passport…?"

But Tania had pretended not to notice her father's tears and had gone silently with the woman in the blue uniform, to end up somewhere near the back of the aircraft, have her seatbelt checked, a rug put across her knees and a kiddies' activity pack handed to her. As the plane lumbered towards a distant runway, her eyelids had grown irresistibly heavy. She just had time to be thankful: any bad dream would be better than sitting wide awake, thinking of her dying grandmother down there among the summer roses, waving goodbye for the first and last time, or her father's wretched attempt to turn her long trip home as an "unaccompanied minor" into one big, jolly adventure. Or the stranger at the airport and the cold bed in a strange school, miles from anywhere, that awaited her at home.

The jumbo had climbed to 37,000 feet, the films had begun, an early dinner had been served and the window screens had been pulled down for the night. Still Tania slept on. The flight attendants kept an eye on her as they passed up and down the aisle, and marvelled at a child's capacity for sleep. Early in the flight they had suggested to the fat man in the seat next to her that he might like to move – "We have two seats together, sir?" – and gingerly rearranged the sleeping Tania to be more comfortable. This solitary child, they agreed while preparing the meal trolleys in the galley, was more silent and scared than most.

Somewhere over the icy mountains of Greenland, Tania began to sob in her sleep. For some weird reason she was knocking on the door of her own house. It felt empty, and hostile. A policewoman wearing a hat opened the panelled door, and invited her in. In the echoing hallway, in the calm tones of adults with bad news, she announced that she was so sorry, there'd been an accident… It was her—

Tania wept herself out of sleep and into a

moment of utter terror – where is she?... what is that noise?... why that screen, those people kissing? – before gradually remembering all she needed to remember. She wiped her eyes on the navy cotton blanket and decided that a nightmare, even one about her mother having an accident, was not a reason to push the call button for help. She didn't fancy professionally soothing words or cuddles from any one of those strangers, the ever-smiling glossy girls and eager, aproned men. But an older flight attendant went by with water for the sleepless and noticed the young girl's staring eyes. She offered headphones, a chicken or pizza meal, a book, games, cards, fizzy drink, water, all of which were declined with a shake of the head. Well, ground staff looking after the child in LA would have to get some food into her, thought the attendant. She knew from the pre-flight briefing that Tania had three hours between this flight and the next.

In the Los Angeles departure lounge yet another woman in the same blue uniform holding a clipboard of papers tried to make Tania feel better. It was going to be a full flight... she'd be one of the first called... she really must have some food, keep her blood sugar levels up... outside, the pollution levels were right up there… Tania thought this minder too big for her uniform, her hair too curly and her accent really weird. She remained silent, knowing they would both be relieved when the boarding call came. *I'm eleven and three-quarters,* she wanted to yell. *I'm not going anywhere. Just… leave me?*

Three hours had turned into seven. Tania had wandered – several times – through the bookshop with its Hollywood mugs and Mickey Mouse T-shirts, past the burger bars and the TV screens and the booths offering cheap Internet. She'd bought, and got halfway through, a novel about girls working on a cruise ship that she'd never want her mother to see.

The last airport minder was toothpick-thin, with severe blonde hair, and smelt strongly of lemons. With departure near, she was trying really hard, repeating niceties first said by the curly-haired one hours ago. "They say it's so beautiful, your cute little country. I just *adored* that *Lord of the Rings*… and *The Whale Rider* and *King Kong* too… Oh, but there's your boarding call now. Got your passport there? They want boarding pass *and* passport these days, ever since 9-11… My, it's a full plane…"

Signed off speedily into Row 47, Seat B and the

care of yet more uniforms, Tania waited fearfully for whoever would sit squashed up on either side of her for the next twelve hours. At least on the flights over she'd had her father's shoulder to sleep on. In the departure lounge she'd seen some really *odd* people. Surfies with nose rings, grannies dressed in gym gear, weird tattooed women in long skirts, men with shaven skulls, several so bulky they were nearly square and waddled. Please God, she prayed, let them all have seats *anywhere* but Seats A or C, Row 47. She watched passengers lurch down the aisle, lugging babies, cabin bags and backpacks, herding young children and their gear – until she decided that relief from this suspense might be temporarily found in the toilet. Trembling slightly, she sat there, on the lid, avoiding her pale face in the mirror. Announcements came booming at her from the Flight Director, thuds distantly from underneath (luggage doors being closed?). Eventually, obeying an attendant's request to return to her seat as they were just about to close up and push back, she unlocked the toilet door. "You OK, sweetheart?" he cooed. "We've asked your nice neighbours to keep an eye."

Having refused all food since Heathrow, she realised she was now desperately hungry.

In the aisle seat was a brown giant, with a pony tail and jeans, with his shoes already off. As he hauled himself to his feet to let her pass, making no eye contact at all, she was aware of his strong smell – not sweat or Italian aftershave or stinky shoes, but something sweeter, earthy. Swiftly, Tania assessed that she could get used to the smell, but his bulk overflowing into her seat when he was asleep might be a problem. Talking, probably not; what would a tough-looking Maori or Indian (or possibly both) with a bone carving dangling from his left ear want to say to a white girl, or she to him.

In the window seat sat a grandma, quite smart as grandmas went. Her blouse was covered with pink flowers, her hair defiantly bronze. As she collapsed into her middle seat and fumbled with the seatbelt, Tania wondered if this old lady would turn out to be a talker, that sort of cosy granny who went on about her garden and her corgi and her grandchildren. Her smile and smell were both welcoming, warm as honey.

"Travelling all alone?" she asked. She had a deep, fruity voice and gold fillings. "What an adventure for a girl! I'm Granny Gloria to my family, so you can call me that too. I pride myself on being a very *modern* granny. And I just *love* meeting new little friends, believe me."

In the briefest of glances sideways, Tania had noticed ropes of pearls and bracelets of silver. Rings on her fingers. She remembered Father's First Rule for Being Left Alone on long flights: start the way you intend to go on. Her father would say, spare me even a modern granny yabbering all the way from LA to Auckland. Say *nothing*!

So she only nodded, and out of the pouch in front of her pulled the airline magazine she had already, over Canada, read from cover to cover.

After an hour in the air, as she watched the meal trolley make its excruciatingly slow progress towards Row 47, Tania was in no doubt that Father's First Rule didn't work with some people. The magazine hadn't worked. Apart from putting on her earphones, or just rudely asking to be left alone, what could she do?

Besides, as she contemplated the mess of empty dishes and torn plastic wrappings on her tray table, Tania admitted that despite herself she had been considerably entertained by the seven grandchildren, exotic travels, the good life in the Lake District – "Ransome country; *surely* you've read Arthur Ransome?!" – before the better life in New Zealand. Granny Gloria, it turned out, was a radio broadcaster, quite famous – she'd covered four Royal tours! Tania thought she must also be what her own granny called "a woman of the world": she had asked to change her meal to the chicken because the lamb was inedible, and for a second mini-bottle of champagne and a second rug, and did they have any slippers, because her feet were cold. And while you're there, sweetie, the latest *Newsweek*? Listening with admiration to these demands taking place over her head, Tania sneaked a look at Seat C, but the large brown man, after eating silently and being helpful handing over food trays, had only once rolled his eyes at Tania in sympathy as Granny Gloria's voice boomed across him, and gone back to reading his book. So far, he'd kept his bulk to his own seat.

Only when Granny Gloria signalled that she was settling down for the night, and she herself was drifting off again, did it occur to Tania that she hadn't been asked a single question about herself, where she lived, or why she was travelling all alone. Perhaps she should just be grateful that for two whole hours she hadn't had to think about it. She'd even found herself laughing a few times; GG really could, as she claimed, "do voices", from the Queen to Bart Simpson.

In the darkened cabin, as GG began to snore and the big man beside her read on under his mini-spotlight, Tania vaguely registered a male voice informing passengers of possible turbulence ahead and the need to ensure that seatbelts remained firmly fastened at all times.

The big man had put out his reading light and Tania was watching the film – Johnny Depp's latest – when somewhere over the equator the jumbo struck the clear air turbulence so disliked by pilots.

A sudden lurch became a violent shudder, followed by a sickening, seemingly endless drop. To sounds of screaming, the plane yoyoed upwards and again viciously shook itself, forwards and back like a rodeo horse, casually sideways.

In less than twenty seconds, nearly four hundred people went from fitful sleep to wide-awake red alert. Johnny Depp disappeared from the screen.

This was why Dad was crying at the airport, thought Tania. *Not because he suddenly had to stay behind and be there when his mum needed painkillers and slowly died – he knew, and I knew too, something was going to happen to my plane.* She had no idea that jumbos, so monumental on the ground, could be tossed around so. No plane could survive this. It was going to be buffeted and shaken and rattled and corkscrewed and yoyoed and broken into thousands of pieces.

She imagined herself strapped in her seat, falling

wide awake and arms flailing, screaming at the top of her lungs, plunging at a million miles an hour thousands of metres downwards through the night into the sea. Sharks would bite by moonlight at the exploded bits of her.

Head buried into her navy blanket, she curled herself up into a ball. Her whimpers became increasingly high-pitched yelps of terror, just like in that rare electrical storm directly over her house in Auckland once, when only her father's arms had saved her from her own frenzy. She had believed the world was crashing to its end, as it was now.

"Hello, little girl." Granny Gloria must have leaned right over towards her, her voice was so loud. "It's only CAT, chin up." This having no effect, she hissed, "Drama queen behaviour is so unbecoming. I've been in worse and believe me, ten minutes – it'll all be over. And CAT or no, nature's calling and must be obeyed. Excuse me."

What's CAT? And the old bag never even asked my name, seethed Tania, as she all but disappeared into her seat to let Granny Gloria, smelling of sour, old-lady sleep, clamber heavily over her. She heard raised, bossy voices, GG's and male, probably an annoyed flight attendant, and then distant shrieks other than her own as a giant paw gave the aircraft a particularly brutal shake before dropping it into another deep hole.

But, even as the wild ride continued and she fought to breathe under her blanket, she knew nothing could change. GG for all her toothy smiles was no friend at all and there were no strong arms available this time.

"Tania?" said a man's deep voice above the roar. "Sometimes I travel with my daughter, Waimoana. She's about the same age as you, and I know what she'd be wanting, eh."

The big man had pulled up the armrest between them. Feeling herself enfolded, her cheek against his padded vest, his earthy smell intensified, Tania found herself gradually relaxing into big shuddering sobs. By the time Granny Gloria noisily required them to let her back into her window seat, although the aircraft was being bucketed around as ferociously as ever, simple human touch had proved itself enough. She even started to feel sleepy. Forty minutes later, when the exhausted passengers realised that this particular CAT had finally let them go and slunk back into its lair, Tania pulled slowly away to rearrange her limbs and her eleven-year-old dignity into her own seat.

A little shamefaced, aware she was being

watched, she realised that she'd only seen him in profile. Even in the dimmed cabin, she could see that full-face, he was more Maori-looking than Indian; his eyes were brown, kind and summing her up. She'd be very annoyed with anyone who tried to tell her that a man, a dad, whatever colour he was, couldn't be kind to other people's children when they needed help.

"What's CAT?" she asked.

"Clear air turbulence." He pulled the armrest back down to its normal position. "I've a friend who's a 747 captain and they all hate it. Severe equatorial storms they can sometimes fly around, or over, but CAT they can't always predict. This little lot lasted a good deal longer than most."

"I'll *never* fly again," she declared.

"Eh, girl?!" he laughed. "Yes, you will. CAT doesn't happen too often. Most flights are smooth as a baby's bottom. But CAT – it scares me too. I've just learned to hide it. You going home?"

"Auckland." And then, because he seemed kind and interested, she wanted to tell him everything. "My dad and I went to England to see my English granny for the first time, but she got liver cancer all of a sudden and he's stayed behind to help her die which might take months and is going to be very painful. So I had to be an unaccompanied minor to get out of the way and back to school in time. I was in LAX for seven whole hours which was horrible."

"It's a horrible airport. Not as bad as it used to be, but still one of the worst. So, your mum's meeting you...?" As Tania's eyes filled immediately with tears, his enormous hand rested briefly on her arm. "Sorry, Tania. That was tactless of me. Just because my own kids have two live-in and available parents doesn't mean I should've assumed you have."

"It's OK. Not Mum – Dad said some person from the school would be there." Suddenly cold, and embarrassed by her initial, hasty judgments, she pulled the blanket up around her neck. "Mum's got an important job in Wellington. She goes there Monday to Friday. *Boarding* school," she added with vehemence, "where I'm being parked until Dad gets back, and probably forever."

"No grandparents at home?"

"They don't want me either. Well, they do, but only for occasional nights when it suits them, and anyway, they like my big brother better than me. What's your job?"

He invited her to guess, and having ruled out anything to do with sport or factories, Tania found herself further embarrassed. She'd heard enough, especially from her Auckland grandfather, of Maori and drugs, crime, truancy, jails, violence, poor parenting, dole-bludging. The big man revealed himself as a barrister who appeared in youth courts. Of course he got scared, he smiled, all the time, not just for his responsibility to his clients, but his responsibility to himself, especially when he walked into that loneliest of places, a courtroom of mostly white faces except for the young people he was defending.

But being alone, he added, could be a positive, beautiful thing, like now; with six more hours to Auckland, neither needed to fill the space with small talk. Far better watch Johnny Depp, and get some sleep. And Grandma, he whispered – take a bet? Having lost her monopoly, Grandma wouldn't trouble her again. Later, over breakfast, when the blinds came up and the bright Pacific sunlight poured in, he'd tell her about Waimoana and her sisters and see how Tania could perhaps, if her parents agreed, visit the family on leave weekends. They had a rambling old house just outside the city, with a couple of hounds and a pool...

"Oh yes, please," said Tania, putting on her earphones. And she would tell him about belonging to the school orchestra and the Maori culture group, and her favourite authors, and her mother's hope that she'd do law too. And that of course she was proud of her mum's important job down in Wellington but wished... just sometimes...

Later, she asked sleepily, "How did you know my name?"

"I heard the flight attendants talking about the girl in Row 47. And I saw it written on your cabin bag in the locker above. Don't tell, but I was a cop once. A detective."

Tania smiled. The credits were rolling on Johnny Depp. All those names, hundreds of them.

But she'd ask the big man with the earring his name when she woke, at daybreak.

The Alien

SUE ANDERSON

LESSON ONE

"Now, listen, all of you!" Miss Pacey was shouting again. Her voice was getting squeaky and she was fiddling with the board pen. I was in the back row, having an argument with Michelle, about crisps.

"I did. I gave you enough for two packets."

"No, you didn't. You gave me…"

"You two in the back row!" She was staring straight at us. "I've a good mind to move you."

"But, Miss," I said.

"We like it here," said Michelle. She's not scared of teachers. Neither am I, really, but charm sometimes works. "We'll be good, Miss. I promise."

Miss Pacey gave me a hard stare. "Well, OK. But you have to listen." Junior and Calum, squashed in the corner, grinned and gave a thumbs-up. We'd won.

"Right," said Miss Pacey. "This is a new project. Early this morning, a spaceship landed on that hill over there." She pointed out of the window. Calum immediately stood up. "Where, miss? At the top?

Hang on, I can see it, that grey thing."

"That's a water tank you fool!" Junior dug him in the ribs. Other kids were joining in now. "Look, it's over there." "No it isn't. I can—"

"SHUT UP!" Miss P had really lost it. Her face was getting pink. Somebody near the door put their finger to their lips. Those of us who weren't completely stupid realised there was danger outside. So it was only Calum who got caught when Mr Hartley, the Year Head, walked in with the stranger.

"Calum. Outside. Now!" he said. "The rest of you listen up. This is Anna. She's travelled a very long way to be here. I want you to make her welcome." The stranger was tall and thin. She had black hair down to her shoulders, not tied back, and she wasn't wearing a proper uniform, just a grey sweatshirt and a raggy-looking blue skirt. She had old-fashioned sneakers, the kind we wore in junior school. I didn't like the look of her at all.

"Now, where would be the best place for Anna to sit?" said Mr Hartley.

"Over there with Michelle and Carly," said Miss Pacey. "They love to chat. They'll help her settle in. Michelle, can you move into Calum's seat? Then Anna can sit between you." Michelle frowned. "Where's Calum going to sit?"

"He can move forward a bit. There's an empty desk over here. What's the matter, Junior?"

"Nothing, Miss." But I knew what he was thinking. Junior and Calum had fought their way through the pack to nab that corner spot at the beginning of term, and now Calum was out in the cold. Michelle gave me a look and I rolled my eyes. It had been great, the four of us together in the back row, passing notes and making jokes. If we were careful, we got away with it most of the time because we were just far enough away from Miss Pacey. Now this stranger had walked in and spoilt our nice little set-up. And to make it worse, she was from some place at the back of beyond. Probably didn't even speak proper English. Actually, she didn't speak at all. She sat looking straight in front, not even trying to smile.

"Carry on, Miss Pacey," said Mr Hartley and left the room. We could see him talking to Calum outside. Pacey set off again. "On the spaceship is an alien creature. Over the next four lessons, we'll be finding out what happens when we come in contact with him. We'll start off with some group work. Each group has to decide on a description of their particular alien, and what the spaceship looks like. Michelle, Junior and Carly, you can be one group. And Anna, of course. Do you understand dear?

The stranger stared at her without answering.

"DO... YOU... UNDERSTAND, ANNA?" said Pacey, as if she was talking to an idiot. We had our hands over our mouths, trying not to laugh out loud. The stranger blinked, like she'd just come awake. "Yes, certainly. I understand good." She had a funny accent. That made us giggle even more.

We pulled our chairs into a circle. Calum came back, looking a bit pale, and we waved to him to come and sit with us so he brought his chair over. Miss Pacey pretended not to notice. I explained about the alien.

"It's really stupid," said Michelle. "Kid's stuff." She got her mirror out of her bag, stuck it on the desk and started doing her hair. The boys were actually getting into the project now, discussing what a creature from outer space would look like.

"I bet he'd be like a huge blob," said Calum.

"With poisonous tentacles," said Junior, "And great big—"

"Hang on," Michelle looked up. "How do you know it's a he?"

"Because females can't drive spaceships," said Junior. Michelle swiped him with her hairbrush. He gave a yelp and Miss Pacey turned and glared at us. The strange girl didn't even blink.

"I bet it's tall and thin," I said, "with long black fur. I bet its top half's grey and its bottom half's blue." The girl gave me a look. Then she suddenly smiled.

"And it has big mouth with potato bits stuck all around." Everybody burst out laughing, while I snatched Michelle's mirror and scrubbed frantically at my mouth with a tissue. That did it. This was war.

LESSON TWO

"OK now, class. Listen." We'd moved the desks round so we could have a drama session. Miss Pacey, now known as Spacey, was running around, trying to get us organised. Each group had to act out a meeting with their alien visitor. That meant we had to choose somebody to play the part. It wasn't difficult.

"Anna should do it," I said. "She'd be perfect." She didn't seem to mind. She stood there while we had a little conference.

"Well, it's pretty obvious what we say, isn't it?" said Calum.

"Welcome to our planet?" said Junior.

"Have you brought us any presents?" said Michelle.

"No." Calum shook his head. "No way. We say,

'Try anything and you're dead meat.' What do you think it's come all this way for? A cup of tea?"

"I'm with Calum," I said. "The alien's a threat. I think we should take it into custody. Make sure it can't do us any harm." I was waiting for a reaction, but the girl didn't speak, just stared into the distance. She really was quite strange.

"Well, I think we should assume it's friendly," said Junior. "Or why would it come on its own?"

"Let's vote on it," I said. "Who thinks the alien's dangerous?" I stuck my hand up as I was speaking. Michelle and Calum did the same. "There you go," I said. I put my hand on Anna's arm. Physical contact was against the rules in drama, but being an alien, she wouldn't know that.

The next thing I knew, I had my hand twisted up behind my back and she was holding me, powerless. I screamed.

"What's going on?" Spacey bustled over.

"She attacked me, miss!" I said.

"Anna doesn't know the drama rules," said Spacey. "We should have explained. NO PHYSICAL CONTACT. DO YOU UNDERSTAND, DEAR?" Anna let me go. The others were grinning. If I'd had a ray gun I'd have zapped them all. As it was, I went and sat down on the bench and refused to do any more drama. Pacey never makes a fuss if you say you're observing. Michelle came and sat with me, but the two idiot boys acted out some close-encounter scenes and creepy Anna just stood there, being an alien.

"I bet she really is one," I said to Michelle. "I bet she really does come from outer space. I'm going to tell my dad and he'll make a complaint about her. She's dangerous."

As a matter of fact, I didn't tell my dad, because something happened on the way home which put it right out of my mind. Me and Michelle were taking a short cut down Kinsley Road. This is always a bit chancy, because there are people down there you wouldn't want to meet on a dark night. The houses are all a bit run down. Quite a few of them have been turned into flats and there are some cheap boarding-houses with oddbods staying in them. Anyway, we were about halfway along, having a serious talk about clothes for the school disco, when suddenly this voice said, "Well, look who it isn't."

My heart sank. It was Serena Brown from Year Eleven. She's awful. She's got a really bad reputation. She's about six foot tall and she bullies people. I usually manage to keep out of her way. I'd never seen her in this part of town though, so it came as quite a shock.

"I know you," she said in her big loud voice. "I've seen you before."

"Of course you have." I was trying to sound calm. "We go to the same school."

She growled at me. That's the only way to put it. She actually bared her teeth. "Think I'm stupid or som'ik?"

"No, I just…"

"Because I ain't stupid. You want to apologise, you do." She took a step towards me. I took a step back. I glanced round for Michelle. There were two of us, after all, and…

Michelle wasn't there. She was heading back down the road as fast as her non-uniform trainers would take her. Michelle is in the running team and it certainly showed. So much for best friends.

So what do you do? I can't run for chocolate, and I certainly can't fight. I wondered whether I could buy her off. Crisps maybe? Then I realised I'd given up crisps ever since that incident with the alien. My bag had nothing in it except a few books. This girl wasn't interested in books. She was near enough for me to see her skin problems close up. She was smiling at me, which was pretty scary. My heart was hammering in my ears.

"Hey. You there!"

The voice came from behind me. I glanced

round. Three people were standing there, all dressed in grey tracksuits. One was a big man with long black hair, tied back in a ponytail. Next to him was a boy. He wasn't very big, but he looked hard. The other one was Anna.

"You, nasty girl," said the man. "Go away. You troublemaker." For a second I thought he was talking to me. But it wasn't me. Serena's face was turning bright red.

"You can't tell me what to do," she said. "You lot have got no business here. You're illegal imulants, you are. You should go back where you came from." But she took a step back. You could tell she was weighing them up and she wasn't that confident.

Then something really weird happened. The man squatted down and Anna hopped onto his shoulders, quick as a flash. Then he stood up and the boy just climbed up both of them, like they were a staircase, and stood balanced on Anna's shoulders. Then the whole lot of them moved towards Serena, towering over her like some great grey monster.

Serena took one look and set off down the street. She was running faster than my so-called friend. I watched her until she was out of sight.

Somebody tapped me on the shoulder and I

looked round. It was Anna, back on ground level. "Are you OK?"

"Yeah. I'm fine. That was absolutely brilliant. How did you learn to do that?"

So she told me.

LESSON THREE

We were playing a game. It was quite good actually. You picked an object in the classroom, just something ordinary. Then you described it to the class as if you were from another planet and you'd never seen anything like it before.

I did the whiteboard. "Flat oblong shape stuck on a wall. Humans make coloured marks on it." Calum did the window. "Screen with moving pictures of green wavy stuff." Junior did a chair. "Brown thing with four legs and a flat bit on top."

Michelle wasn't there. She'd been off school for a week. Her mum rang mine and said she was suffering from stress. Mum had a go at me, but I said I meant every word of what I'd said to her and she deserved it.

It was Anna's turn next. "DO YOU WANT TO TRY, DEAR?" said Miss Pacey and she nodded. I was fairly sure Anna wouldn't have any trouble. She'd always understood English pretty well, but she was much better at speaking it now. She'd had loads of practice. She'd been spending quite a bit of time at our place. It got her away from that awful flat the housing people had put them in – just a couple of damp rooms with a kitchen that smelt of mould.

The family were all circus performers – acrobats. How cool is that? They came from some country I can't even say, let alone spell. Anna's dad showed us on an old, tatty map he'd brought with him. The writing was funny, all strange shapes and squiggles, but I could see it was right at the far end of Europe.

They were hoping to get permission to stay here. Anna had been part of the team – she got to dress up in a sparkly costume and climb ropes and do somersaults and stuff. Until somebody set fire to their caravan and they had to run for it. You wouldn't believe the things they'd had to put up with, trying to get away. It made Serena look tame.

Anyway, here she was, standing up in front of the class, ready to do her talk. "Go for it, Anna," I whispered, and she did.

"These animals come in many colours and shapes. But they are really very much same. They all have one head and four limbs. They all speak with mouths and have eyes and nose. They can be very fierce to strangers, but they are good to their friends. They all have one heart." Then she sat down. Everybody was quiet for a minute and then Calum said, "That was brilliant. Better than mine." And Miss Pacey (who is now one of my favourite teachers) said, "Well done, Anna. That was very good indeed."

LESSON FOUR

We were back in our group again. This time we were making a farewell speech to our alien, and we had to give it some presents. Michelle had come back. At first she was a bit catty to Anna, but I told her about the circus stuff and she changed her mind. Michelle admires physical fitness and she's a sucker for sequins.

All the other groups had brought stupid things for their alien, like packets of sweets and horror comics. But we had some real presents. We had photos of all four of us that we'd done in the photo booth in town. And we had a beautiful blue cotton sweatshirt. And my mum had baked a fruitcake. We'd hidden them in Miss Pacey's cupboard, so Anna didn't know.

We got to perform our farewell scene in the hall, last lesson on Friday. The other groups were quite good. One lot had a green alien costume with antennae that kept falling off. One group had made a spaceship with cardboard boxes. Some others had brought in a space hopper, and their alien jumped away on it and fell off the stage. (It was all right though – it was Darren and his head's like concrete.)

We didn't do costumes. That was my idea. "Who says aliens have to be different?" I asked them. "Perhaps they'd look just like us." And even Michelle agreed it was a good point.

I got to make the farewell speech. I said, "Thank you for coming to our planet. We need to know that our way is not the only way to live. We learnt a lot from you and we'll miss you very much." Then, after a bit of scrabbling, Michelle came up with the presents.

Don't laugh, but I choked up a bit. Michelle's mascara had gone runny, and even Calum had something in his eye. Junior was staring very hard at the ceiling.

Our alien didn't cry. She had that calm expression on her face again, but I wasn't fooled. When she first came I used to think it was because she didn't care, but now I know it's when she's fighting the tears back. She said, "Thank you very much for the wonderful presents. I have learnt a lot from you also. I have learnt that I can make friends in a strange place. I don't know where I will be going in the future, but I promise to keep in touch."

We haven't seen our alien for a while. The family were moved and we don't know if they've been allowed to stay. Anna promised she'd write and I haven't heard, so I'm worried. But sometime, somehow, I'm sure a message will come.

I'll just have to keep watching the sky.

Eve Goes First

Sarah D. Bunting

It seems like it takes forever to get out of the house – out of her room where she's carefully arranged some lumped-up sweaters under the covers to look like her sleeping self; down the stairs, way on the left side to keep them from creaking; through the front hall and through the front door, opening and closing it like a thief so the tongue of the lock falls silently into place. It really only takes about five minutes, but Bailey has never snuck out before and stark terror is messing with her sense of time.

Melanie is waiting at the end of the front walk. She's got a backpack on that's so full of stuff, she looks like an astronaut, and she's staring up at the second floor and shaking her head.

"Hi," Bailey says. "… What?"

Melanie points at a second-floor window, and when Bailey looks, she sees her little brother Toby in the window, smiling smugly.

"Twerp alert," Melanie says. She whips a mitten off to give Toby the finger, but Bailey stops her. "No no no no don't, he'll tell for sure… Shoot, do you have five dollars?" When Melanie hands it over, Bailey holds it up to Toby, opens a hand, and mouths, "Five. Bucks."

Toby glares.

Bailey glares.

Toby mouths, "OK." He sticks his tongue out at Melanie and then his head disappears.

Bailey sighs. "God. Sorry. OK, you ready?"

"Yep." Melanie jerks her mitten back on. "Let's get this over with."

The plan is to walk down Evergreen Road, cut through the gardens behind the Fortnightly Club, and come out on Dawson Avenue across from the older part of the cemetery. The Fortnightly Club is where the old men in their town go to smoke smelly cigars and complain about their achy bones, but the old men in their town go to bed early; the club's windows are dark.

Bailey and Melanie walk in silence for a few minutes. Bribing Toby has put them a few minutes behind, but they can still make it by 11.45 if they keep moving. It's the first really cold night, scarf-cold, and the air seems to carry the little sounds better – leaves rustling, twig snaps, the rattling of Melanie's backpack.

"Mels, what is that?" Bailey says. "You're like a human maraca."

Melanie yoinks her backpack around on her back to identify the sound. "I think it's a box of Tic Tacs. You want one?"

"I want them to shut up. Shut up, Tic Tacs."

"'Sor-reeee, Bay-leeee,'" Melanie says, in the voice of the Tic Tacs, and Bailey laughs, but it sounds really loud in her ears, and anyway she feels weird laughing, tonight of all nights. She rubs her hands to keep them warm, and without speaking, Melanie hands her one mitten. Each of them puts both of their hands together in one mitten, praying-style, and they walk along that way until they get to the Fortnightly Club, where they stop.

Melanie says, "They don't have an *alarm*, right?" and Bailey says, "Guess we'll find out," and hops over the property line.

"Alarm-free!"

"Unless it's silent," Melanie says, following Bailey.

"Well, why would the Fortnightly Club have an *alarm*? To protect their valuable..."

"... cigars," Melanie says. "'I'm quite fond of this cigar, I must say, it tastes like a shoe I had in the war—' OW!" They've got to the edge of the property, to the wooded public land, and Melanie's just taken a branch to the face.

"Jeez, are you OK?"

"Yeah, I've got another eye. Stupid branch," and Melanie breaks it off angrily.

It's hard to see back there in the thicket. They can hear the occasional car on Dawson Avenue, but the branches above them block out the moonlight, and the trees and the dead leaves on the ground blend together into a field of dark brown. Bailey remembers a path from their daylight dry run, but she can't find it now, and low-hanging branches keep grabbing Melanie's backpack.

"These trees ah eeeee-vil," Melanie says in a movie-villain accent, but she's not really joking.

"Well, maybe if you hadn't brought your entire room," Bailey says, yanking a dead vine out of the zipper for her. "What have you got in here, anyway?"

"You know. The books, extra batteries, a canteen, *CosmoGirl*—"

"Tic Tacs…"

"Many, many Tic Tacs."

"Many *angry* Tic Tacs."

"Twelve angry mints," Melanie says, and then she stubs her toe and says, "Whatever, *tree stump*," really angrily, and Bailey is laughing again, so hard she almost can't stop. She has to stand still for a minute and just giggle while Melanie and her backpack get into fights with nature.

Finally she calms down and wipes the giggle tears off her cheeks with Melanie's mitten. They feel cool and refreshing on her face.

"It wasn't *that* funny," Melanie says, spitting out a leaf.

"It was pretty funny," Bailey says. "Plus it was something…" She trails off. Melanie looks out towards the road and finishes for her: "Something Eve would say."

"Yeah," Bailey says.

"I was thinking that, when I said it," Melanie says. "That it was weird, that I said it just then." She squinches both hands back into the mitten. "Did you think it was weird?"

"Funny, mostly," Bailey says. "You know what, it reminds me of when she kicked Timboo." Last year, this kid Timboo annoyed their class every morning by standing up by the blackboard, bending over, and making his butt talk, until one morning Eve walked in and said, "Whatever, *Timboo*," and kicked him in the butt, which obviously everyone in Mr Runcik's classroom had wanted to do for months, but nobody else had the guts. Timboo fell over, and he got really mad about it and called Eve "Steve" for the rest of the year for some reason, but at least he stopped with the butt-talk after that.

"Ha, that was awesome. The best part was how she just kept walking to her seat."

"That *was* awesome. I don't know how she didn't start laughing hysterically."

"Or get in trouble."

They come out onto Dawson Avenue. No cars are coming by; just a few leaves roll past, pushed by the breeze.

Bailey takes a deep breath and lets it out. "Whatever, Dawson Avenue," she says, but very quietly.

"Yeah," Melanie says, also in a whisper, and checks her watch. "Eleven forty-six. So, if we... want to go back? And not do it?"

"We can't," Bailey says firmly.

"No, I know, but if—"

"Why, do *you* want to? Go back?"

"No, I'm just saying if *you* did? We should do it now. Before we..." Melanie gestures at the cemetery fence.

Bailey sighs. "We have no choice, Mels." She looks both ways and starts to head across the street. Melanie hikes up her backpack and frowns.

"No choice, right... Right."

They have no choice because they've already tried everything else. First, they tried a Ouija board, but that didn't work, and actually they got into a fight about it because each one accused the other of moving the triangle doodad on purpose, which they both denied doing at first and then both admitted because neither of them had wanted the other one to be disappointed. Then they held a séance, but that didn't work either; Melanie thought it was because they had used a Glade scented candle, instead of a plain white one like Bailey's book suggested, but Bailey blamed Toby, who was eavesdropping as usual. Leave it to Toby to block the portal to the spirit world.

Next, Bailey read up on spirit recording; some of these paranormal-society people claimed that you could press "record" on an ordinary tape recorder and invite the spirits to communicate, and the spirits would talk on the tape and you could play it back later. So they thought they'd try that, but they had to leave the tape recorder at the cemetery on their way home from school, and the tape always ran out before it even got dark. After the third time they'd listened back, and heard nothing but Ken the caretaker's lawnmower, again, Melanie said maybe they should give up, but Bailey thought they should try once more, in person – at midnight.

It's nearly midnight now. Dawson Avenue is deserted. It's so quiet, Bailey's ears ring with it.

She almost hopes for a car or a barking dog, but the town is completely silent, like it's watching them, holding its breath along with them, to see if Eve comes.

The girls just walk right in through the south gate and onto the neatly trimmed grass.

"So, OK," Melanie says. Her voice is unsteady.

"This way," Bailey says, like she's giving an order, thinking of what her dad told her before she had her appendix out, that it's not brave if you're not afraid, thinking of Eve kicking Timboo, thinking of how Eve would have run ahead of them. Eve would always do it first of the three of them, whatever the "it" was, even when the "it" was scary.

Especially when the "it" was scary.

Bailey strides off down the path, through the older section with the nineteenth-century graves all furry with moss, soft and strangely friendly-looking. Melanie rattles along behind her. To pass the big Dominski mausoleum, they have to walk through its shadow, and in the middle of the shadow, Melanie puts her arm through Bailey's and bends her elbow down hard like she's literally locking her arm onto Bailey. Bailey bends her elbow hard right back.

"Feels colder," Melanie says. "Colder than back outside. Do you think it's… that?"

"No," Bailey says. She knows what Melanie means; the books say that when you come near or walk through a ghost, you'll feel an intense cold, like it comes from the centre of your bones. "I think it's just windier on this little hill up here."

"But the wind isn't. Blowing right now," Melanie says.

"Never mind," Bailey says. She's concentrating, looking for the Griswold headstone that will tell them to turn right and shortcut over to the newer plots.

At last, they find it. Bailey feels strange about walking right over the graves, but it's that or stay on the path, and they don't have time for that; it's only a few minutes until midnight. They hurry along, both of them counting off the plots. Twelve, thirteen, fourteen. Here.

Eve's grave.

They stand at the edge, looking at the big pinkish marble block that Eve's parents picked out. The grass is still new, frail. Melanie stretches out her foot and grooms the sod with her sneaker toe, erasing one of Ken's bootprints.

"OK," Bailey says, "let's see the tape recorder."

Melanie wiggles out of her backpack and digs down to the bottom, past the magazines and Tic Tacs, and produces the recorder.

"I put fresh batteries in earlier."

Bailey takes the tape recorder and cradles it like a baby in one arm. It's heavy, and she doesn't want to hold it the whole time but she isn't sure where to put it down. After a minute, she just centres it at the foot of the grave. She's about to press "record", but she hesitates.

"What?" Melanie says.

"If she doesn't come, we can try again another night," Bailey says.

"OK," Melanie says, and raises her eyebrows.

"And if she *does* come..."

Melanie rolls her eyes. "If she *does* come, we have to talk to her first, so that she can talk to us, blah blah, I read the book, I know."

"No, I know you know," Bailey says. "I just..." She feels a corner in her throat, a corner of tears she has to swallow around, and it makes it hard to talk. She has to force the question out, around the corner: "What if I don't know. What to say."

Melanie says, "It's Eve. You'll know what to say."

"But what if I don't have time?" Bailey's eyes are leaking now, but she doesn't care. She's too scared. She's not scared of the trees rustling and talking amongst themselves all around, or of getting caught when Toby tattles on her, which he totally will even with the five dollars. She's scared of Eve's ghost, because even if she remembers to say everything she's saved up to say all this time, how she misses Eve like a broken bone, how she still saves the gross black liquorice jellybeans for Eve, who likes them, how nothing is as funny anymore and she and Melanie are lonely even when they're together sometimes, even if she says all of that and begs Eve to come back... what if all that comes out is "goodbye"? She said that already. They both did. Nobody answered.

Melanie grabs her hand. "She'll know what you mean."

Bailey flicks a tear off her cheek. "She will?"

"*I* know what you mean," Melanie whispers, and she bends down still holding Bailey's hand and presses "record" and stands back up and says in a shaky voice, "If anyone has anything to say, please, speak to us!"

This is what the books told them to do.

"Speak to us!" Melanie says again.

The wind picks up a little, just a gentle shushing noise above them.

"Speak to us!"

Then Bailey is cold, very cold, like a block of ice is in her stomach trying to get out, she's desperate to get warm so she grabs Melanie and hugs her as hard as she can, the wind is blowing and stinging her eyelids where the tears are still drying, and Melanie hugs her back and says, "Speak to us!" over and over again and squeezes Bailey too tight for breathing, and Bailey feels empty, like she's falling, like she's in her bedroom again on her bed highlighting *The Scarlet Letter* and her father comes in looking like he's holding his face onto his head using his jaw muscles, and he tells her there's been an accident, Eve's been in an accident, she felt the same way then, falling, sitting on her bed and falling, falling into herself like an abandoned house, empty and cold, goodbye, goodbye.

"Bailey! Bailey!"

It's Bailey's mother. She's storming across the grass, right across the plots in her dressing gown, furious, with the police on her heels. Toby has told on them, and Bailey is grounded and so is Melanie, possibly forever, or at least that's what Bailey can make out; she's exhausted and headachy and happy just to sit in the back of the police car and warm up and not hear. She and Melanie sit there with the tape recorder between them on the seat, watching Bailey's mother talking to the cops, listening to the scratch and burst of the radio, and when Melanie's dad pulls up in his Volvo, Melanie and Bailey exchange a look.

"Whatever, *Dad*," Melanie says, pulling her hat

down over her eyes.

"Whatever, *Toby*," Bailey says, shivering, and she and Melanie exchange a look, and Melanie reaches down and presses "rewind". The tape whirrs for a while and then clicks, and stops.

"Speak to us," Bailey whispers, and presses "play".

Author Biographies

Sue Anderson is a teacher who works with teenagers who won't go to school. They teach her a lot. Her favourite books are mostly science fiction and fantasy. She lives in Wales with two cats, Buffy and Willow, who keep the vampires away.

Sarah D. Bunting is co-editor-in-chief of televisionwithoutpity.com and editor-in-chief of tomatonation.com; she is also the author of *The Famous Ghost Monologues*. She's fascinated by unsolved mysteries. You can find her in Brooklyn, New York, probably in a coffee shop.

Marcia Byalick is a family-issues columnist, a content editor of beinggirl.com, and the author of three novels for young adults. She has two daughters, and enjoys the pleasure and challenge of writing for the world's most sophisticated audience – perceptive, savvy young women!

Tessa Duder trained as a journalist and had four daughters before becoming a writer and editor of books for both children and adults, including two award-winning series for young adults. She lives in Auckland, New Zealand, and counts sailing, square-rig ships, music and reading among her interests.

Jamila Gavin has been writing for children for over twenty years. She enjoys finding stories for all ages, from six to sixteen, and her childhood, spent in both India and England, has given her a very rich soil to till. Her novel *Coram Boy* was Whitbread Children's Book of the Year in 2000.

Libby Gleeson has won many awards for her picture books and longer fiction for children and young adults. She grew up in rural Australia and subsequently lived in both Italy and England. She has three daughters, and now lives in Sydney, Australia.

Julia Green lives in Bath with her two teenage sons. She is the author of *Blue Moon*, *Baby Blue* and *Hunter's Heart* (Puffin). She has lots of best friends! Julia lectures in creative writing at Bath Spa University.

Belinda Hollyer lives in London, where she has a cat-shaped hole in her life, and in Key West, where she shares a cat called Minnie Mouser. She grew up in New Zealand, lived in Australia for several years, travels as much as possible, and dreams of islands, tidal rivers, and Africa.

Angela Kanter lives with her husband and two daughters, in a very untidy house on the edge of London. When she was at school, she had quite a cool Saturday job on a kids' radio show, but now she just sits in a newspaper office drinking coffee all day. She has published two books for children.

Shirley Klock and her husband serve as staff for two Norwegian Elkhounds in the San Francisco Bay area. Her story "Snow Globe Moment" appears in *Like Mother, Like Daughter?* (Kingfisher). Other short stories have appeared in *Cicada* and *Cricket* magazines.

Sophie McKenzie lives in London and works as a freelance editor when she isn't writing books. Her first children's novel, *Girl Missing*, was published by Simon & Schuster in 2006. "T4J" is her first short story.

Lois Metzger has written four novels and many short stories for young adults. She lives in New York City with her husband and teenage son.

Norman Silver was born in Cape Town on the slopes of Table Mountain. At the age of 23 he left South Africa and has lived in England since then. His publications include novels, short stories and poetry for teenagers. His current project is www.txtcafe.com.

Frances Thomas has written several books for children, as well as two adult novels. She lived for many years in London, but has now moved to Wales, where she enjoys reading, walking and looking out of the window.

Acknowledgements

The publisher would like to thank the copyright holders for permission to reproduce the following copyright material:

"The Alien" copyright © **Sue Anderson** 2006; "Eve Goes First" copyright © **Sarah D. Bunting** 2006; "Under the Influence" copyright © **Marcia Byalick** 2006; "Taking Flight" copyright © **Tessa Duder** 2006; "The Gardener's Daughter" copyright © 2006 **Jamila Gavin**; "Annie and Me" copyright © **Libby Gleeson** 2006; "Make Friends, Make Friends, Never Never Break Friends" copyright © **Julia Green** 2006; "The Middle Ground" copyright © 2006 **Belinda Hollyer**; "Dear Meena" copyright © **Angela Kanter** 2006; "Speaking Esperanto" copyright © **Shirley Klock** 2006; "T4J" copyright © **Sophie McKenzie** 2006; "Silence" copyright © **Lois Metzger** 2006; "The Swing Chair" copyright © **Norman Silver** 2006; "Toad Crossing" copyright © 2006 **Frances Thomas**.